DEEPHAVEN

Also by Ethan M. Aldridge

Estranged

Estranged: The Changeling King

The Legend of Brightblade

DEEPHAVEN

Ethan M. Aldridge

Quill Tree Books
An Imprint of HarperCollinsPublishers

Quill Tree Books is an imprint of HarperCollins Publishers.

Deephaven
Copyright © 2023 by Ethan M. Aldridge
All rights reserved. Printed in the United States of America.
No part of this book may be used or reproduced in any manner
whatsoever without written permission except in the case of brief
quotations embodied in critical articles and reviews. For information
address HarperCollins Children's Books, a division of HarperCollins
Publishers, 195 Broadway, New York, NY 10007.
www.harpercollinschildrens.com

Library of Congress Control Number: 2023932458
ISBN 978-0-06-328316-9

Typography by Torborg Davern
23 24 25 26 27 LBC 5 4 3 2 1
First Edition

*To my siblings, Erika, Hannah, Cole, and Megan,
and all the strange stories we've shared over the years*

Chapter One

The great house reached out with the shadow of its spires, welcoming Guinevere Tallow with a cold embrace. Deephaven Academy had greeted many such children in the past, but today its silent affection was reserved only for Nev. They shivered at the touch and pulled their customary dark green coat tighter around their shoulders.

They never went anywhere without that coat, though it was clearly too big for them. The hem reached nearly to their knees, and its rough fabric had a comforting weight. Its many pockets were perfect for the various odds and ends that Nev was forever picking up. They'd even stitched on a few extra pockets. Beneath the coat, they wore a clean collared shirt and dark slacks that were looking a little rumpled after the long trip by train and truck, and a pair of narrow black boots. They'd purchased the clothes with the last of the money they'd hidden away, after paying for their train ticket. The small tan suitcase in Nev's hand was their only luggage. There hadn't been time to pack more; Nev had needed to leave home in a hurry.

They stood in the leaf-strewn drive of Deephaven Academy, listening to the sounds of the old truck that had carried them from the station fade into the distance, until its rumbling cough was indistinguishable from the shush of the forest leaves. It had been a long drive, more than an hour from the town where the station was located. The driver had been waiting for them there. She'd given Nev a grim nod when they showed her the letter from the school before ushering them into the truck. They hadn't talked much along the way. Instead, Nev had watched silently as the autumn-soaked forest slid past the truck's grimy windows.

Standing now in the far-flung valley, surrounded by trees and silence and evening mist, towered over by the hulking mass of the great house, Nev felt even smaller than they usually did. They ran their hand through their short dark hair, which still curled at the edges from the recent unfamiliar cut.

A new haircut, a new outfit, a new life. They'd transformed themself on the way to Deephaven Academy, slipping into a shape more comfortable than the one they'd known. Nev intended to seize this chance, here in this mist-shrouded valley where no one knew them or all that had happened before. Here, they could be the person they needed to be. This was Nev's chance to finally feel comfortable in their own skin, a chance to start over. Probably their only chance.

It had been an easy choice to leave everything behind and accept Deephaven's invitation. Nev's mother had vanished years before, toward the end of the Depression, unable to cope with the tiny apartment in the crowded city with too little money and too much need. After she'd gone, Nev's father had fallen apart in a different way. He threw what little money they had left into get-rich-quick schemes and bad deals with worse people, anything that made him feel like escape was just one lucky break away. All it got him were empty pockets and angry men pounding on their apartment door. It all finally collapsed, and Nev didn't have anything to keep them home.

They took a deep breath and started for the front

door of the looming house.

Deephaven looked exactly like the photo in the pamphlet Nev had received along with the letter, but in person there was something *off* about it. The house was as sprawling and stately as had been advertised. Tall, narrow lattice windows ran along each of its floors, glinting gold in the late-evening light. Old stone and peaked roofs, even a few scattered gargoyles along the corners, leered dimly out of the gathering gloom. The pamphlet had said that the school was built around what remained of a historic chapel, and it certainly looked like it.

What hadn't been visible in the academy's pamphlet was how crooked the place was. Nev had a careful eye for how things fit together, and the house *didn't*. Corners didn't quite match up, or they ran at odd angles. It made Nev feel dizzy, as if the house were coming apart in slow motion, sinking unevenly into the surrounding earth.

As their eyes took in the ancient edifice, their attention was caught by a figure in a high window, watching Nev's approach.

Nev froze, gazing up at the shadowy silhouette. They couldn't make out any details through the rough window glass, but the figure looked large. Its edges were tangled and ragged, bleeding into the shadows of the house behind it. Not knowing what else to do, Nev gave a small wave.

The shadow behind the glass didn't move. It simply continued to stare down at them. Its stillness was so absolute that Nev began to doubt that the shape was even a person. Perhaps it was a piece of furniture, or the ragged reflection of a tree in the surrounding forest. Nev shuddered and quickly continued forward, feeling invisible eyes tracking their every step.

The front door was an imposing thing, dark wood wrapped in huge bands of iron, a clear holdover from the house's chapel days. Nev knocked, smarting their knuckles on the stiff, cold wood. The sound reverberated heavily into the space beyond.

Then there was only silence.

Nev was a day early; the academic term wasn't starting until tomorrow. They had written the school in advance to let them know about their premature arrival, and while they hadn't received a response, there *had* been someone to pick up Nev at the train station.

Nev waited a few more chilly moments, then tried the door's imposing iron handle. It *was* a school, after all. It wasn't as if they were barging into someone's private home. Besides, Nev reasoned, they were a student there. They belonged. That's what the letter said, anyway.

The letter had arrived with the stack of usual bills and late notices addressed to their father, all of which Nev meticulously sorted. Seeing their name spelled out in a looping, handwritten script on the front of the envelope had been a surprise. It had been awhile since someone had sent them a letter.

It had contained a pamphlet, extolling the virtues of the prestigious Deephaven Academy, an image of the grand house displayed on the front. It was a small school, catering to a very select crowd of "talented and promising students." Looking over the included list of notable alumni, it seemed that "talented and promising" mostly meant "rich." They'd even heard of some of the people: famous artists and politicians, scientists and engineers. An impressive school, and one far above what Nev could ever hope to afford.

But then they had read the letter that had come with the pamphlet. And then read it again, sure they'd misunderstood its message. It was an offer for a full scholarship, room and board included, granted to them in recognition of their "prodigious talent and clear potential." It was signed by the principal of the school, Susan Blanchly. Nev had turned the whole packet over and over, sure it had been sent to them by mistake. Of course, it's hard to address something to a name like "Guinevere Tallow" by mistake.

Nev had put the letter away. Their father needed them at home, not away at some mysterious boarding school. Every day had the same shape; they would wake up early and check if their father was sleeping the night off somewhere comfortable, if he had bothered to return home at all. Nev would then head to the small park near their smaller apartment, claim a spot along a well-trodden path, and spread out a colorful patchwork blanket to display the little toys they'd made to sell. Clockwork mice and windup rabbits, trinkets sold for souvenirs. It wasn't much, just enough to keep the landlord at bay and food in the pantry, most of the time. In the evening they'd return home, sleep, and do it again the next day.

Plans, of course, changed.

The door to Deephaven opened surprisingly smooth. Nev looked along the outside wall of the house, trying to see if the figure from the window above was still watching, but the window was out of sight, hidden behind the strange angles of the house.

Nev stepped out of the cold and into the matching cold of the house's wide foyer, the high ceilings and long stone floor putting them in mind of the church this place had apparently once been. A massive rug, its pattern worn and faded from the passage of untold students, lay along the floor. The walls were set with gas lamps, each emitting a low hiss, warm light flickering through their fogged glass bulbs and bathing the floor in an amber glow.

Nev blinked in the dim light. The apartment they'd lived in had electric light for as long as they could remember, though they supposed the technology hadn't quite made it out to the more far-flung parts of the countryside. Something about the honey-tinted glow of the gaslight settled their nerves a little.

Dark-wood doors lined either side of the hallway and two sets of stairs flanked the far end, winding up into darkness. Set above the arched stone doorway Nev had just passed through was a detailed carving of a symbol that Nev recognized from the pamphlet as the school's crest: a shield emblazoned with an open book, a twiglike wand with a single leaf still attached resting across its pages. In elegant script over the shield were the words *"Potentiale est Potentia."*

"Um, hello?" Nev called.

Their raspy voice echoed around the cavernous space, swallowed by the halls until the house repeated it gently back to them.

"Hello . . ."

Nev shivered, feeling silly. Why were they cowering in the entryway, waiting for some adult to materialize and take their hand? They straightened their shoulders, gripping their small suitcase with one hand and digging the other into their coat pocket, and set off deeper into the house.

Empty hallways branched like veins through the house, eventually leading Nev to a circular, comfortably furnished sitting room. It had a cold fireplace and a staircase winding up along the wall and out of sight to the floors above.

Small tables in the sitting area held books and vases, most covered in a thin layer of dust. The flowers in the vases, however, looked fresh. It was the first sign Nev had seen that they weren't the only person to walk these halls in months.

They stepped closer to examine them, finding an open sewing kit next to a vase, colored threads and rows of long needles packed inside. Without really thinking about it, Nev picked up a large silver bobbin from the box and slipped it into the inner upper-right pocket of their coat with a practiced motion. *Just in case*, they thought. They always thought this when collecting.

Nev turned back toward the sprawling emptiness of the house, and at the end of the far hall, they saw a ghost.

Chapter Two

Nev's heart stuttered. The thin white thing glided smoothly down the hall toward them, stepping out of the gloom. No, not a ghost. A girl. A tall and slender girl with a pale face, pale hair, a white jacket, and a cream-colored skirt. She stared at Nev with wide green eyes in an expression of surprise that mirrored Nev's own.

The girl's face split into a sudden grin. Something about the look of that smile put Nev in mind of a picture they'd seen in a book once, of a crocodile who'd just spotted an antelope on a nearby shore.

"You're early," the pale girl said. She nodded

toward the sewing box where Nev had just taken the bobbin. "Picking up a souvenir for your first day?"

"I-I'm sorry," Nev said, feeling their face flush.

Their collecting habits had got them into trouble more than once. Nev was normally very careful about where and when they picked things up, but they made mistakes sometimes, and the habit had gotten worse over the years since their mother left. They never knew when they might need something, in case they never got a chance to have it again.

"I wrote to say that I'd be here," Nev continued, hoping to change the subject. It would feel weird to try and put the bobbin back now. "There was a person waiting for me at the station, so I thought . . ." Nev trailed off.

"Oh, you met Martha!" the girl said, delighted. "She's a bit quiet, but she's lovely. The academy hires her to run errands from town and pick up students every so often. She's one of the only people in town with a motorcar, you know. The principal must have alerted her to our early bird."

She stuck her hand out, her slender fingers extended for Nev to take.

"And your name is . . . ?"

Nev shook her hand, trying to muster what they hoped was a confident grip.

"Guinevere Tallow," they said.

"You're serious?"

Nev shrugged. It was a reaction they were used to.

"My mother taught classical literature, and my great-great-grandfather was a candlemaker, or something like that. You can just call me Nev, if you like."

The girl's grin grew improbably wider.

"Well, Deephaven *certainly* has a type. My name is Patience Sleepwell."

Nev stared at her for a moment, trying to decide if they were being teased somehow. They didn't think so.

"Come with me," Patience said, her pale hair cascading elegantly as she turned. "The principal will want to know you've arrived. And don't worry about the souvenir. That sewing box has been sitting there for as long as I've been at the school."

"You can leave that here," she added, nodding to Nev's suitcase. "The dormitories are just above, so you'll be coming back this way anyhow."

Nev left their suitcase on a nearby armchair before scurrying to keep up with Patience's long strides. All that was in the suitcase were a few blank notebooks and spare shirts and trousers. Anything of any real importance was in their jacket pockets, as always.

"You've had a chance to look around the house?"

Patience asked as they walked. She linked arms companionably with Nev, pulling them along in their stride. "What do you think?"

"It's, ah, big," Nev said, as they passed back through the entry hall where Nev again saw the school's crest.

"What does that mean?" they asked, pointing to the Latin inscription.

Patience didn't turn around.

"*Potentiale est Potentia.* Potential is power. Language is a specialty of mine. Don't worry, Latin is one of the first things they teach you here."

Patience led them to the staircase that curved around to the left, making her way as confidently as someone who'd lived in the house for years. Nev huffed, feeling a little out of breath from all the twists and turns.

"You'll get used to it," Patience said, "and it won't feel so empty once the rest of the students arrive. My father wasn't sure about sending me to school in the middle of nowhere, but I got my way. What about your parents? The send-off wasn't too tearful, I hope?"

"My parents are gone," Nev said, and it was even true, after a fashion. They'd repeated a version of this line to several people over the last few days as they'd made their way to the secluded New England valley where Deephaven Academy rested.

Instead of showing the typical look of sympathy, Patience merely nodded at the statement.

"Sometimes that's best. In my experience, they tend to be in the way more often than it's worth. You're here now, and that's the important thing."

Nev frowned. It seemed like an odd thing to say, though they couldn't help but agree.

"So," Nev said, trying to be personable. It had never been their strong suit, but this place was meant to be a new beginning, so it seemed like a good time to try new things. "How come you're here early?"

"Oh, I didn't leave," Patience said. "I've been here over the summer to help keep things running."

This surprised Nev. They looked up at the girl, who was nearly a head taller than them, and only a couple of years older at most.

"By yourself? Why?"

Patience winked at them.

"We've just met, Guinevere. You'll have to get to know me better before I tell you all of my secrets. For now, all you need to know is I'm one of the prefects at the academy; it's my job to make sure the students are well settled and to keep everything running."

"Is there anyone else here right now? To help you keep things running, I mean," Nev said. They thought about the ragged shape that had watched their arrival from the high window.

"The principal is often around during the summer, but not always. Apart from her, I'm the only one here. And now you, of course."

The stairs wound higher as they talked, passing small landings and shut doors, the passage dark except for the occasional gas lamp set into the wall above them. After an exhaustingly long climb, the stairs leveled out at a landing, bigger than the ones they'd passed, set with two simple wood chairs and a side table with an unlit candlestick, flanking a narrow, shut door. There were no gas lamps installed there, and Nev blinked into the darkness.

"Wait here while I announce you," Patience said. "I hope you're not afraid of the dark; I don't have anything to light the candle."

"That's all right," Nev said, reaching into their inner middle-left pocket. They drew out a small book of matches that they always kept there, just in case, lighting the candle on the small table.

Patience beamed.

"Resourceful. I like that," she said. "I think we're going to be great friends, Guinevere."

With that, Patience gave three sharp knocks on the door, waited a moment, then opened it and slipped inside. Nev caught the smallest glimpse of a warmly lit space and densely packed bookshelves before the door closed and left them alone on the candlelit landing.

Nev settled into one of the chairs, the wood hard and uncomfortable beneath them. They stared at the nearby candle flame, which burned unmoving in the still air. They tried to listen through the thick wood door, but they couldn't make out the words, the house sighing around them and obscuring the sounds.

Their nervousness began to bleed back into them, and their hands fidgeted nervously in their pockets, turning over the small screwdriver and needle-nose pliers in their outer lower-left one. The tools hadn't seen much use lately; there hadn't been time to work on new toys. Nev itched to make a new one, to have the calming satisfaction of fitting something together. They wouldn't need to sell them on their little quilt in the park anymore, assuming nothing went horribly wrong.

Which, they supposed, it still could.

Patience emerged at last from the room, flashing Nev a reassuring smile and holding the door open. Nev stood, smoothed the lapels of their jacket, and stepped inside.

The room was small, lined with the same dark wood as much of the rest of the house. The same bookshelves that Nev had seen from the outside

17

crowded in around them, filled with not only books, but carved wood boxes, framed certificates, and various other artifacts. A single narrow lattice window was set into one wall, overlooking the forested hills that surrounded the house. In front of the window hunched a desk, the same dark wood as the walls, its surface packed with books and papers in meticulous piles.

Sitting behind that desk was the most terrifying person Nev had ever seen.

"You're Guinevere Tallow," Principal Blanchly said. It wasn't a question, but Nev nodded anyway.

"Take a seat."

Principal Blanchly was a narrow woman, all long limbs and hard angles. Round, silvery spectacles glinted above sharp cheekbones, and she had a pinched mouth set in a permanent expression of suspicion. Her ink and granite hair was pulled back so tightly it made Nev's scalp ache just looking at it. She wore a charcoal suit with sharp, unforgiving shoulders, giving her a family resemblance to the gargoyles that lined Deephaven's rooftops. Her long, bony fingers gripped a fountain pen, poised to strike over a ledger open in front of her. She leveled steely gray eyes at Nev over her spectacles, and though Nev knew they had just been invited in, something in that piercing gaze made them feel as if they had just done something terribly, unforgivably wrong.

Nev slid into the small chair in front of the desk, trying not to fidget as Blanchly's attention returned to the ledger in front of her. For a time, there was only the insistent scratching of pen against paper, and the distant, dreamy mumbling of the house. Nev's gaze drifted around the room, snagging on various objects: a large handbell made of dark metal sitting on the desk, a purple geode on the shelf with an almost person-shaped hollow in the middle, a daggerlike letter opener balanced on the edge of a stack of books. Nev's fingers itched, but they controlled themself. People didn't look kindly on their habit of collecting, and Nev needed to make a good first impression.

Finally, Principal Blanchly finished her writing with a flourish and closed the pen with a sharp snap. She leveled her steely eyes at Nev again, and Nev had to resist the urge to flee.

"I trust you were able to find your way without difficulty," the principal continued. Again, though the words implied a question, her tone made it very clear that it was not. "I am Principal Susan Blanchly. Welcome to Deephaven Academy."

Nev felt the house shiver through their boots in answer to its own name.

"Thank you," Nev said. They tried to force their voice out clear and confident, and they were reasonably satisfied with the result.

"As you will have already been informed, Deephaven is *very* selective of its student body. You are one of the few students who have been offered a scholarship this year. I hope you grasp the enormity of the opportunity that has been extended to you."

"Yes, ma'am," Nev replied. "Principal Blanchly, I was wondering . . ."

They trailed off, not knowing if the question was rude. They didn't want to risk their place at Deephaven. Options otherwise would be *very limited*.

Blanchly said nothing, waiting for Nev to finish.

"I was wondering," Nev said, "*why* I was offered a scholarship. If I might ask, that is."

Blanchly continued to stare at them, her eyes studying Nev's face, her expression giving no clue as to whether she was satisfied with what she saw there.

"Something that you should learn now is that I will never mince words with my students," Blanchly said. "I am not here to coddle egos or spare feelings. I am here to teach, and to provide the structure needed to shape the young lives of my students. You, Guinevere Tallow, were offered a scholarship because you simply could not afford to attend this academy otherwise. Certainly not with the pocket change you earned from that little toy shop of yours."

Nev stiffened.

"You know about that?"

Blanchly pulled open a narrow drawer, never taking her eyes from Nev, and withdrew a small red object, placing it on the desk. It was a mouse, made of clockwork and red canvas. A woven green ribbon served as its tail, and a brassy windup key gleamed from its back.

"Your *business*, let's call it, is a large part of what attracted the academy's attention to you in the first place," Blanchly said. "We at Deephaven value ingenuity and resourcefulness, and we believe these little constructions display those attributes in you. You did make this yourself, didn't you?"

Nev nodded silently. They had a mechanical mind and magpie instincts. The toy mouse's red canvas "fur" had been made from a moth-eaten curtain they'd found in the garbage behind a theater. The clockwork interior that would make the mouse run in circles when wound up had been cobbled together from the pieces of various watches. Nev had many more of the little gears, along with an impressive collection of windup keys, nestled comfortably in their inner middle-right jacket pocket.

21

They remembered the red mouse. They'd set the toy out along with the others to sell on the little quilt by the side of the park road. Nev didn't remember who had bought the red mouse. They certainly felt they would have remembered someone who looked like Principal Blanchly, though.

"Deephaven goes to great pains to scout out some of the most promising young minds, so that we might give them the best opportunity to expand on their potential. While you study here, *you* are expected to take an active role in the expansion of *your* potential," Blanchly said, tapping the mouse's windup key with a single long finger. "This academy has made a significant investment on your behalf, and we will expect a return on that investment."

"Yes, ma'am. I understand," they said.

"Let me be clear," Blanchly said. "You are expected to perform to the utmost of your ability. Anything less, and your scholarship will be terminated and you will be sent home."

Nev met Blanchly's gaze. There was no glimmer of sympathy in the principal's steely gray eyes.

"I won't let you down, ma'am," Nev said, and they meant it. They knew they wouldn't have a home to return to.

"No," Blanchly said, "I don't expect you will."

She pulled open another desk drawer and drew out a small, gleaming object, placing it in front of Nev. It was a brassy, metallic pin, inlaid with a dark green enamel, depicting an open book and an overgrown wand: the crest that Nev had seen above the entryway.

Without another word, Blanchly took up her pen and returned to scratching in her ledger. Their meeting apparently concluded, Nev took the pin and slipped out of the room.

It took some time to find their way back to the dormitory tower, having lost all sense of direction in the labyrinth of Deephaven's halls. They were eventually guided by the smell of food, warm and rich, and Nev followed it like a thread through the maze. It led them back to the sitting room, where Patience waited with Nev's suitcase and two sandwiches of roasted chicken and tomatoes.

"I thought you'd like a little dinner," Patience said with her radiant smile. "It's nothing like what you'll normally have here—Deephaven employs an *excellent* chef, Lin. She's famous in culinary circles, supposedly. But since she doesn't arrive until tomorrow with everyone else, you'll have to make do with me."

Nev had only eaten a roll on the train earlier that day. They tore into the sandwich with enthusiasm. While they ate, Patience, who'd only nibbled at her own food, told them about life at the academy.

"It's a small school," she was saying. "Apart from the principal, we have two full-time professors. There's Professor Bellairs, who teaches History of Alternative Societies, Study of Languages, and Creative Writing, and there's Professor Tieran, who teaches Innovations in Biology and Theoretical Mathematics. She's also the school nurse, should you need. Principal Blanchly does a weekly lecture for the whole academy, and we sometimes get guest experts to come teach more specific courses for a semester or two."

Nev swallowed a mouthful of sandwich. "That all sounds . . . complicated."

Patience smiled. "The classes are *specialized*, let's say. That's why it's such an exclusive school. Don't tell me you aren't up to the challenge?"

The way she said it felt like a dare. Nev was suddenly overcome with the fear that they would disappoint the dazzling prefect, though they didn't really know her.

"I'll figure it out," Nev said, with more confidence than they felt.

Patience winked. "Good."

After Nev had eaten, Patience led them up the winding staircase to their room. They passed door after door, each of them identical, as they spiraled upward. Patience opened one of the doors on the third landing, revealing a small, square room. It was just large enough for a desk, a wardrobe, and a comfortable bed with a heavy quilt covered in a stitched ivy pattern. A single narrow window looked out on the road leading into the forest valley.

"You get your own room," Patience said. "Professor Tieran says it's good for study. Something about the 'monastic life of a true scholar.'"

She gestured to the desk.

"You'll find plenty of paper and ink in there. I turn down the lamps at ten o'clock every night, so there are spare candles in the top drawer in case you need a late study session. Any clothes you need cleaned are sent to the washroom using the service lift one floor below you. If you need anything else, you can ask either me or the other prefect, Thaddeus."

She winked at Nev.

"Between you and me, Thaddeus is terrible and you should avoid him at all costs. Just come to me."

"Thank you," Nev said. "And thank you for the sandwich."

At the sight of the bed and the welcoming green expanse of the embroidered quilt, it hit Nev how incredibly tired they felt. It had been a very long, very hard couple of days.

"My room is just on the floor above," Patience said. She took Nev's hands in her own, smiling that friendly, hungry smile as she pulled them close. "I'm *so* happy you're here, Guinevere. You're going to fit in perfectly."

Chapter Three

Dusty sunlight streamed in through the narrow window of Nev's room as a busy hum was already filtering up through the floorboards. The sound was familiar, though it still made Nev nervous; the rambunctious noise of the first day of school.

Nev peered out the window and saw a stream of motorcars and carriages pulling down the dirt road through the valley toward the house. The cars looked shiny, like beetles in the late-morning light. They all pulled around the drive at the front of the school, where Nev lost sight of them.

It took a long time for Nev to work up the courage

to step out of their dormitory. They tried to stall by unpacking, though since they'd brought so little, this didn't take up nearly as much time as Nev would have liked. Eventually, compelled by a combination of the tempting smells of breakfast floating upstairs and the increasing rumble of their stomach, Nev resigned themself. They smoothed their still-curling hair as best they could, buttoned on a fresh shirt, and slipped into their customary, comforting coat, the gleaming emerald crest of the academy now fixed to the lapel. Nev stood, bouncing on their heels with hands stuffed in their pockets, for a brief moment before darting forward and stepping out the door.

They were immediately swept up in a tide of students cramming themselves up and down the narrow, spiraling dormitory stairs. They wore every color and trim of smart suits or skirts, and the only thing linking them together was the glint of brassy metal and emerald enamel shining from their collars or lapels. There was no prescribed dress code at Deephaven; students simply had to wear the pin. Above the students' heads they hefted bulging bags and bulky trunks. The students shouted back and forth to each other: greetings, insults, invitations, negotiations. Nev stumbled back a few steps up the stairs, pummeled both by the students and the sound.

Eventually, Nev was able to make their way out of the worst of the crowd and out into the wider house. From there, they roamed the halls in search of the dining room, trying to follow the smell of breakfast.

The large dining room had been laid with an array of small, circular tables, surrounded by high-backed wood chairs. A long row of tall lattice windows lined one wall and looked out on the drive. Only one of the tables was occupied by two boys, each in dark tweed suits, tearing into plates of eggs with their luggage still resting by their ankles. One boy looked up and gave Nev a perfunctory nod before returning to his breakfast.

Nev returned the favor, striding past the boys' table toward the breakfast spread nearby. It was full of trays of food: steaming biscuits and fresh fruit, covered plates hiding fresh eggs and stacks of sausage. Curving porcelain pitchers wafted the scent of tea from their spouts. Trays were occasionally refreshed by a pair of students, who appeared out of a door next to the spread, presumably leading to the kitchen and the famous chef.

Nev, who still felt the pangs of hunger from the last few hectic days, took a little bit of everything. They carried their plate to a distant corner of the room and sat under one of the windows painting dusty streaks of light in the morning air. Nev let the sun warm their back through the green fabric of their coat as they chewed happily in silence. So far, so good. They had gained a foothold in the academy and no one had appeared to tell them it had all been a big mistake and that they'd have to go home after all. They pocketed the second fork of the set laid out on the table, just in case.

It would still be some time before the only seminar of the day, by Principal Blanchly, was scheduled to begin. The students were to take the bulk of the day to unpack and get things in order before the start of class-proper the next day. Having already unpacked, Nev knew they should head back toward the dormitories and introduce themself to some of the other students. It would be wise to become an essential piece of the school's machinery as it built the life they hoped to lead.

Still, Nev couldn't make themself go back to the roiling chaos of students. After finishing their breakfast, they picked a door at random, wandering off into the halls until it was time for the principal's opening lecture. Nev reasoned that they were becoming familiar with the bones of the school. After all, it wouldn't be wise to get lost on the way to classes.

They wound their way back and forth, in and

out of rooms set for classes, set for study, or simply crammed with sheet-shrouded furniture. The steady drone of students soon gave way to the gentle grumbling of the house itself. And suddenly, nothing looked familiar, and Nev was certain they'd found their way into one of the house's sprawling wings that they hadn't passed through yesterday. The air felt still and muffled, the goings-on in the main part of the house buried in layers of wood and stone and dust.

Nev breathed deep and tried not to feel like they were hiding. They ran their hand over the beveled details that ran along walls. The lacquered wood felt solid under their hands, a thing that had been there for generations before Nev had arrived and would likely remain for generations after. The house felt like it was a whole world away from the uncertain one of the tiny apartment they shared with their father.

The last time Nev had been in that apartment, they'd been standing in the short hallway that threaded past the bedrooms and led to the tiny kitchen. As angry voices reached through the front door, Nev had frozen, their breath caught in their throat even before they had begun to call their father's name.

It had happened before. Loan sharks and shady business partners coming to collect what Nev's father couldn't possibly pay, the money already sunk into some other doomed scheme. If the men were particularly angry, sometimes Nev's father would be carted off to a little jail cell until he could pay his debts or, more often, Nev managed to scrape together enough change from selling their clockwork toys to pay his bail.

The voices out in the hallway had been angrier than usual this time, and Nev had shut their eyes against it. When the pounding on the apartment door started, Nev could only stand and listen until the door broke down.

They were startled out of their thoughts and pulled back to the present by an unexpected small, melodic ringing. They drew their hand back and saw that they had brushed against the end of a long rope strung with small bells.

The rope was draped across a door and had been nailed firmly to the doorway on either side. Nev reached out and touched one of the silver bells again, ringing it, confused as to its purpose. Was it to ensure students didn't intrude? If so, wasn't the heavy-looking padlock enough?

As the ringing faded, Nev became aware of another sound beneath it: a distant, soft sobbing. An anxious chill bloomed suddenly in Nev's gut. They stood still, trying to pinpoint the source of the sound. They'd almost managed to believe that they'd imagined it when the muffled sound of crying came again.

Nev stared at the door. It had the look of a thing that had been shut with the intention of never being opened again, an air of permanent and purposeful abandonment. Nev leaned in closer, pressing their ear to the cool wood.

The sobbing was continuous now, low and steady. There was a strange quality to the voice, breathy and strangled, as if the throat making it wasn't used to the sound. Nev swallowed, then knocked softly.

"Hello?" they said, their voice quiet. Nev had the feeling that they were not supposed to be here, that they were intruding on something.

The sobbing cut off suddenly, and the house lapsed into its usual groaning silence. Nev tried the door handle, though as expected, it was locked.

"Hello?" Nev said again, forcing their voice louder. "Are you all right?"

They pressed their ear to the door again. No more sobbing came from the other side. Instead came the sound of steady movement.

Tak-a-tak-a-tak-a-tak—

The noise was slow and scratchy as something

shambled steadily toward the door.

Nev was seized by a sudden terror. They had no desire to see what was making the unsettling sound. They pulled back, scrambling away from whatever was clattering toward them on the other side, and ran directly into a boy.

The boy carried a massive stack of luggage in his arms, and though he was broader than Nev and taller by at least a head, he was knocked off-balance by the teetering weight. He and the luggage went spilling across the hallway with a terrific crash.

"Ow," the boy said.

The boy had black, tightly curled hair that was cut close at the sides, and brown skin that contrasted his light cream-colored shirt. He wore dark gray trousers with red suspenders, attached to which was the crest pin marking him as a Deephaven student.

"Sorry—" Nev managed, still feeling shaken. They tried to listen past the noise of the settling luggage, but no sounds of scratching or sobbing came from behind the nearby door.

Nev offered a hand to help the boy up, though he was so much bigger than Nev that they didn't feel like they made much difference.

"That's all right," the boy said, grinning. It was

the smile of someone who seemed genuinely glad to see them.

"It's probably my fault anyway," the boy continued as he straightened his shirt.

"I daresay it was," came another voice, clipped sharp.

A different boy strode around the corner, the wood soles of his finely polished shoes clacking against the floor.

This new boy had sharp cheekbones, pale skin, and piercing blue eyes. His dark hair was slicked back, the color complemented by the finely tailored tweed suit he wore. With his air of assumed authority, Nev knew immediately that this was Thaddeus Cuttingham, the other prefect Patience had mentioned, and had warned them to avoid.

Thaddeus picked up one of the smaller pieces of luggage, turning it over to inspect with a critical eye. With a disgusted click of his tongue, he tossed it to the curly-haired boy, who only just managed to catch it.

"You're lucky that my valise was cushioned by your ribs, otherwise I'd have had you scrubbing toilets for the rest of the semester," Thaddeus said. He turned that same critical eye on Nev, sizing them up.

"You're not supposed to be here, you know," he

said. "The east wing is off-limits to students right now. It's not *safe*."

"Not safe how?" Nev said. They tried to keep their voice civil—it didn't pay to get on a prefect's bad side so early in their stay—but they'd known enough people like Thaddeus to know that it was unlikely that he even *had* a good side.

"It's unstable," Thaddeus said. "One of the floors collapsed. A student was *killed*." He leaned in closer to them, his voice lowered, his expression secretive. "They say it's haunted."

Nev thought of the sobbing from behind the door and couldn't stop the shiver that ran up their spine.

"Now, both of you, get this mess straightened up while I go find another first-year, one with decent stamina," Thaddeus said. He strode past them, the sharp *clack* of his shoes marking his path long after he was out of sight.

The curly-haired boy sighed, turning to struggle with the largest trunk in the pile.

"Here, I'll help," Nev said, feeling guilty for knocking him over. They scrambled to grab the other side of the trunk to help the boy lift, straining under the surprising weight. Nev wasn't known for their upper body strength.

"Thanks," the boy said, steering the trunk to rest

neatly along one wall. "I'm Danny Harper, by the way."

"Guinevere Tallow."

Danny's eyebrows shot up as he reached across the trunk to shake Nev's hand.

"Neat," he said.

"Call me Nev, if you want," they replied. They hefted a bulky canvas bag, which Danny took from them to place on the stack.

"I don't want to delay you from whatever you were doing. I'm sure you're busy with your own errands," Danny said. "You're a first-year like me, right? Prefect Thaddeus said all first-years have chores to do at the beginning of the semester. Part of our duties, I suppose."

"I, ah, hadn't heard that," Nev said, starting to understand the circumstances in which they had run into Danny. The boy looked confused for a moment, before the realization sank in that he had been taken advantage of.

"Oh," was all he said.

There was a long moment of deeply uncomfortable silence, which both of them filled by busily continuing to stack luggage.

"So," Danny said eventually, "how did you hear

about Deephaven?"

"I, ah, I got a scholarship," Nev said, feeling self-conscious. Having had a good look at Danny and most of the other students pouring into the house, it was clear from the cut of their clothes and the weight of their luggage that nearly all of them came from money. Nev was starting to feel shabby in their secondhand coat.

"Wow, congratulations!" Danny said, oblivious to Nev's discomfort. "My dad sent me here. He doesn't like me being in the way during busy work seasons, and an investor friend of his recommended the academy."

He straightened up, casting an uncertain glance around the dim hallway.

"It's definitely out of the way," he said.

"What does your dad do for work?" Nev asked, placing another piece of luggage on the pile, hoping that this was how small talk worked.

Now Danny was the one who shifted uncomfortably. "He works in real estate, kind of," he said. "What about your parents?"

"They're gone," Nev said. For a split second, the last image of their father played in their head, the pleading, betrayed look in his eyes as he was dragged out of the apartment. Nev shook the image from their mind.

"Oh," Danny said.

Neither of them said anything else as they finished assembling the stack of luggage.

"Well," Nev said finally, "I guess I'll see you at orientation."

"Yeah, see you," Danny said, his smile lighting up again. "Good to meet you, Nev."

Nev was already halfway down the hall by the time the words finished leaving his mouth, trying to put as much distance between them and the awkward social encounter as possible.

The house grumbled around them, dreaming of a time when it had been home to more than lonely children. At the very edges of their hearing, Nev thought they heard again the steady scratch of something, far behind the locked door.

Chapter Four

As the evening gloom gathered outside and the sounds of settling within the house began to quiet, Nev followed the flow of students to the central nave of the house. They weren't a large student body, but they were of a wide variety. Nev heard a range of accents, several of which they couldn't place.

Principal Blanchly stood on the raised, altar-like section at the far end of the hall, towering over the students as the other professors at the school stood nearby, chatting amiably with each other.

Nev stayed at the rear of the room, pressed against a cold stone wall. They spotted Danny nearby, talking to a short boy with long black curls framing his brown face and wide, skittish eyes. The boy said something that Nev couldn't hear and Danny laughed, something he seemed to do readily. Nev envied him a little, his ability to make such quick connections with the people around him. It was a skill that Nev had never mastered.

Shepherding the flock of unruly students were Patience and Thaddeus. The two prefects corralled the crowd within the room, casting steely glances at each other as they worked. Nev caught the clash of competition in those looks, saw how they both vied for the obedience and adoration of the other students. Thaddeus was sharp and intimidating, while Patience was all honeyed smiles and light laughter. She glanced up to catch Nev staring and winked. Nev drew back farther into the shadows against the wall.

Principal Blanchly suddenly brought her hands together in a single, sharp clap. The room fell instantly silent.

"*Potentiale est Potentia,*" the principal began, her precise voice cutting through the sudden silence. "Potential is Power. These words are etched over our door. You each carry them upon your person. They are part of our crest, and they form the foundation of this academy. Potential, *your* potential, is the engine that drives this world. It is the power by which we shape our lives and the lives of those around us."

Her gaze swept across the room, taking in each and every student.

"It is the aim of Deephaven Academy to expand on that potential. We will ensure that it reaches its utmost, that your potential *becomes* that power. But to do that, you must make a choice. Do *everything* it takes to become someone worthy of such power, or don't and fail. The choice is yours."

Even as far back as Nev stood, when Blanchly's gaze found theirs, it felt like an accusation.

"This is your chance," the principal continued. "This is a new start. For those of you who are returning students, it is my hope that this year can be an opportunity to recover from . . . the recent tragedy."

This provoked a static sound of whispers from the assembled students. Danny looked around and caught Nev's eye with a quizzical expression.

"Last year's accident left us all shaken. But I will assure you as I've assured your guardians, every measure is being taken to make sure it doesn't happen again. I am certain you will all settle comfortably in the new dormitory wing, and I must insist that no one enter the east wing until repairs are complete. The best way to honor Ms. Wharton's memory is to stay safe, work hard, and remain focused."

Nev returned Danny's glance. They had thought that Thaddeus had been lying to them earlier about the east wing, just trying to scare the new students, but it seemed there was some truth to it after all.

The principal concluded her orientation speech and dismissed the students for the night. The silence she had commanded was immediately shattered by a tide of excitable chatter as students began to crowd out of the central nave and head toward the dormitories.

The immediate return of the chaotic crush made Nev anxious, and they kept to their shadowy corner as tightly as they could while they waited for the crowd to thin. Their fingers twitched nervously, hungry for something to occupy Nev's mechanical mind. They spied a silvery fountain pen, abandoned and forgotten, resting on a nearby side table. They picked it up and slipped it into their inner upper-left pocket, just in case.

They froze when they noticed another student watching them, a girl with dark, silky hair and a finely tailored skirt and jacket. She had an amused smirk on her face as she watched Nev. They flushed, embarrassed at having been caught indulging their bad habit. Nev quickly ducked out of a nearby side door, away from the other students and their judging eyes.

Nev decided to wander until most of the others

had gone to their private rooms, hoping to avoid more awkward encounters. Their plan was ruined almost immediately when they turned a corner and saw Patience, her head bent toward another student in hushed conversation.

"What did you tell her?" the girl said, her voice strained. She had long dark hair, worn so that it covered most of her light brown face and draped over a voluminous knit sweater.

"What am I *supposed* to tell her, Ruth?" Patience bit back, her icy tone freezing Nev in place. "I told the principal what she needed to know."

"This isn't right," the other girl said. "This isn't *helping* anything. You said you'd fix this."

"You say that like it's easy," Patience said. "I've done what I can, and now you need—"

She cut off suddenly as her eyes found Nev's in the gloom. For the smallest of moments, Nev saw a burning rage flare across her face, before it was replaced by the shine of her brilliant smile. Nev felt suddenly embarrassed, having been caught eavesdropping on the prefect's private conversation.

"Guinevere!" Patience said musically. The other girl flinched visibly, turning to look at Nev with the expression of a startled deer.

Patience gestured Nev closer.

46

"This is Ruth. She's an old friend of mine. Ruth, this is Guinevere, one of our promising new recruits."

Ruth nodded from under her veil of hair, uttering a small noise that might have been "hi."

"Hello," Nev said. "Um, sorry, I didn't mean to interrupt—"

"It's fine. Ruth and I were just discussing a school project from last year. Nothing important."

Ruth scowled, or Nev thought she did for what little they could see of her expression.

"Is there something I can help you with, Guinevere?" Patience asked sweetly.

"No, I was just— No. I'm sorry, I guess I'm just feeling a little restless."

"Understandable on your first day," Patience said, "but you'd best be heading to your room. I'm off to turn down the gaslights for the evening. Trust me, you don't want to be lost in the halls after dark."

Nev nodded, turned, and hurried back the way they came, guarded silence and careful stares burning behind them.

❦

Boom, boom, boom!

Nev startled awake. Panic flooded their sheet-tangled limbs as the pounding at their bedroom

47

door continued. Nev tumbled out of bed, scrambling around in the dark for their coat.

Boom, boom, boom!

Nev drew the coat over their nightshirt, fastening the top few buttons before drawing back the bolt on the door.

Prefect Thaddeus stood on the landing, carrying a small candelabra. He wore a spotless pale linen suit and a crocodile grin.

"Good evening," he said. "Tallow, isn't it? Come along, you're late. The others are already waiting."

Nev blinked rapidly, their sleep-muddled eyes dazzled by the candlelight.

"Others?"

"The other first-years!" Thaddeus said, as if talking to someone particularly slow. "It's time for your initiation. You might want to bring a candle."

Without another word, Thaddeus turned on his heel and clacked down the winding dormitory stairs.

Nev hadn't heard anything about an initiation. Patience certainly hadn't mentioned it, and everyone seemed to avoid Thaddeus whenever possible. Still, he was a prefect, and Nev couldn't risk getting on his bad side so early in the semester. They dressed and grabbed a candle from the desk, screwing it into a small holder. They stepped quickly down the stairs, following the sharp clack of Thaddeus's heels.

The house murmured sleepily to itself as the two traveled through its silent hallways. The place was transformed in the dark, a shadowy labyrinth that defied any mental map Nev had constructed. All they could do was follow Thaddeus's confident strides. Even though they lost all sense of direction, Nev wasn't entirely surprised when they ended up in front of the bell-strung door to the east wing.

There was a small group of other students already there, each of them looking as confused and drowsy-eyed as Nev felt. There was a girl with fluffy hair and a long nightgown, yawning into a large woven shawl wrapped around her shoulder, and the skittish boy with large eyes that Nev had seen Danny laughing with at orientation. Nev's heart sank to see the tall girl with silky black hair, the one who'd caught them "collecting." With them stood Danny, wrapped in a vibrant blue robe over his pajamas and, improbably, a sword strapped to his hip.

"Well," Thaddeus said, bringing his hands together in a sharp clap. "As an academy prefect, it's my duty to ensure that you are all properly settling into life at Deephaven. You've had a chance to see the professors and meet your fellow students. Now it's time to pay your respects to the *local* residents."

He stood there, hands held primly behind his back, soaking in the confused silence that followed, pointedly waiting for a question.

After a long moment, the tall girl obliged with a tired sigh. "Residents?"

"The students who came before you, but found themselves unable to leave," Thaddeus said. He nodded to the door. "They reside here now. And they demand the respect of newcomers."

Danny blinked blearily at the door.

"I thought . . . the east wing was unsafe, that no one lives there."

Thaddeus smirked.

"'Living' isn't exactly the right word for what they do," he said.

The small, squirrelly boy made a frightened *meep* noise. The tall girl scoffed.

"Did we really get dragged out of bed in the middle of the night to hear a ghost story?" she said.

Thaddeus *tsked*. "I wouldn't use the *g* word. It upsets them."

He turned to the door, grasping one of the large iron nails that held the bell rope to the frame. The nail was apparently loose, because it came free easily after Thaddeus wiggled it back and forth. His movements were slow, careful to avoid ringing the bells.

He set the bell rope on the ground and drew out a ring of keys from his inner jacket pocket.

"You are to keep the residents company until sunrise," Thaddeus said. He separated a small key from the ring and slotted it into the impressive padlock that held the door's bolt shut.

"D-do the professors know about this?" the small boy stammered, taking a few stumbling steps away from the east wing door. Nev wondered the same, and if Patience had known about this and had chosen not to tell them. They weren't sure if the prefect and professors knowing about this late-night "initiation" made it worse or not.

Thaddeus flashed another grin.

"Principal Blanchly gave *me* the authority to oversee the students at the academy. What I say goes. If you'd like, I'm happy to tell the principal that you've decided to ignore honored Deephaven traditions. Or, perhaps, that I caught a couple of first-years creeping around after bedtime to do who knows what? Some of you already have a reputation for sticky fingers, after all."

He glanced meaningfully at Nev. They kept their expression neutral, but Nev felt their face flush.

Thaddeus's imperious gaze swept across them all. "So, what will it be?"

The first-years shared a glance but didn't say anything.

"Good," Thaddeus said.

He twisted the key in the lock and a deep *thunk* resonated through the door, sending a shower of dust drifting from its frame. Thaddeus pulled the door open and gave a showman's sweeping gesture into the sooty darkness beyond.

"After you."

Nev stared into the dark, trying to make out the shapes within, but the east wing ate up what little light was cast from Thaddeus's candelabra. A strange smell drifted out of the opening; among the usual scent of dust and stale air common to abandoned places, there was a slight sharp tang like burned metal, iron and bloody.

Danny put his arm around the small boy, who had begun to shiver violently.

"Come on," Danny said reassuringly, "it'll be all right. It's just a game."

He strode with the boy past Thaddeus and into the dark without sparing a glance at the prefect. Nev followed, and the tall girl and the shawl-wrapped student trailed behind.

"I'll be back to collect you at sunrise," Thaddeus said. "Be nice to the locals. They spook easily."

Thaddeus gave a self-satisfied chuckle as he closed the door. It locked with another heavy *thunk*, leaving the first-years alone in the dust-choked darkness.

A strangled yelp came from one of them in the sudden inky black. Nev fumbled in their inner middle-left pocket for the book of matches, bringing one hissing to life and lighting the candle they'd brought with them. The circle of warm light cast from the candleholder's polished back illuminated the space around them.

It revealed a room very much like the one at the bottom of the dormitory wing, with an empty fireplace and a winding staircase twisting up to unseen floors above. The room was filled with mismatched furniture, all of which was destroyed. Couches and chairs lay toppled or smashed, their upholstery shredded and scattered across the scarred wood floor. A thick layer of dust settled over everything, giving the space a muffled hush, like a city after snowfall.

Nev held out their light, spreading the flame to the candles the other students had carried from their rooms. The amber light did little to dispel the heavy gloom, but the deepest shadows flinched back from the huddled students. They grouped their candles together, forming a fragmented campfire in the middle of the room.

"This isn't so bad," Danny said. His tone was

cheery, though Nev thought they could hear a note of tension.

"I was just tossed out of bed by a boy with an over-blown sense of self-importance," the tall girl said. She crouched on the floor in such a way as to be touching as little of the ragged ruins as possible. "I'm now hud-dled in a freezing structural hazard in the middle of the night. It's bad enough."

They all sat in uncomfortable silence, listening to the house.

"So, I've met Nev and Beckett," Danny said finally, nodding to them and the small, wide-eyed boy. "And I'm Danny Harper."

"Agnes," said the shawl-wrapped girl with a yawn.

"I'm Victoria Barker," the tall girl said, with a tone that suggested she expected them to recognize the name. Her irritation deepened when none of them did.

"Do you think it's true?" Beckett squeaked. Even sitting bundled on the floor, he was attempting to maintain his shelter under Danny's broad shoulders. "Do you think the east wing is really haunted?"

"I heard it's haunted by that girl, the one who died in the accident the principal talked about," Agnes said. "The floor collapsed and she got stuck, buried under all the wood and stone. They say she was there for three days, crying the whole time. They tried to dig her out, but they were too late."

Nev shivered, remembering the sounds of sobbing they'd heard from the other side of the door. They tried to distract themself by studying the surrounding space. Something about the inside of the east wing bothered them, nagging at their sense of something being out of place, but they couldn't put their finger on it.

"That's horrible," Beckett whispered.

"That's nonsense," Victoria scoffed. "Do you think this school would have been allowed to stay open if a student had *died* here like that? It would have been a major scandal, all over the papers."

The group nodded in agreement, but none of them looked very convinced, not even Victoria. No matter how skeptical someone is, it's far too easy to believe in ghost stories when standing in dark, abandoned places.

"I think we'll be safe as long as we all stay on the ground floor," Danny said. "Safe from another collapse, at least."

"Oh, are you an expert in building collapses?" Victoria said nastily. "I suppose you must be. I bet you learned all about how to tear things down from your daddy."

Danny went still. An icy gleam appeared in his

eye, freezing out his usual warm demeanor.

"His dad?" Agnes said.

"Mr. Harper Senior makes a business of wrecking homes, doesn't he, *Danny*? He knocks down houses and parks and puts up his ugly little apartment buildings. He fills them with anyone willing to live in a shoebox and makes a fortune. Isn't that right, Danny?"

Nev remembered Danny saying his father worked in real estate. They also remembered he was uncomfortable when saying it.

Danny's expression was frigid.

"Don't," he said slowly, "ever talk about my father to me again."

Victoria's smug expression slipped at his icy tone, her eyes darting to the inexplicable sword hanging from his hip.

"How do you know all that?" Agnes asked.

"Oh, I hear things," Victoria said, eager to maintain control in the conversation. "*My* daddy is a famous actor; you've probably heard of him. Tobias Barker? Well, anyway, he's a big donor to several charitable causes, including developing poor neighborhoods. Mr. Harper has been at several of our dinners; he's *very* friendly with all the big donors. It's funny, I've never seen Danny at those dinners, though I *did* hear the Harpers had adopted a stray."

"There's no sign of a collapse," Nev said suddenly. They desperately wanted to change the tense subject, and they'd finally realized what had been bothering them about the room.

"What?" Beckett said.

"Look," Nev continued, shining the directed beam of light from their candle around the space. "There's no rubble, no sign of construction or repair. The floor above us looks intact. No one has even tried to clear out the things that are still usable. It's just abandoned."

Nev shone their light around the floor, taking in more details now that they knew what they were looking for. Apart from the ruined furniture, the only other sign that something bad had happened was deep, ragged gouges in the wood and stone around the locked door. Something about the look of those gouges made Nev feel cold.

"Maybe the collapse happened higher up in the tower?" Agnes said, looking around with renewed scrutiny.

Victoria scoffed at Nev. "Casing the joint, are you? Aren't there enough things for you to steal in the rest of the house?"

Now it was Nev who went still.

"You're being mean, Victoria," Agnes said reproachfully.

"What? I *saw* them do it," Victoria said. "I heard they stole the silver in the dining room too, just squirreled it away into that raggedy coat of theirs."

"They don't steal," Danny said defensively. He glanced at Nev, who was careful to avoid looking at any of them.

"Your last name is Tallow, right?" Victoria said to Nev, ignoring Danny. "As in, *fat*? It's a name I haven't heard before, and I know all the important names. Where are you from, Tallow?"

Nev ignored her, still shining their light around the place, looking for signs of the missing collapse.

"I suppose you're one of the academy's charity cases," Victoria continued. "I think that's very nice of the principal. It's important to allow poor people an opportunity to improve themselves, even if they steal."

Nev stood abruptly, taking their candle and striding toward the stairway that curved upward into the abandoned tower.

"Where are you going?!" squeaked Beckett.

Nev didn't turn around. "To steal things," they said.

Chapter Five

The first thing Nev saw at the top of the stairs was bones. They shone pale in the candlelight, scattered like leaves across the dusty floorboards. Nev hesitated, feeling like a clenched fist was squeezing their heart, as they wondered if going off on their own had been a terrible idea. They knelt down, bringing their candle close to the nearest cluster of bones.

They were small, seemingly the scattered remains of some animal like a squirrel or rat that had lived in the surrounding woods and had gotten stuck within the abandoned wing of the house. Nev let out a relieved breath in a *whoosh* that almost extinguished their candle, trying to ignore just how many bones there were.

Contrary to Agnes's guess, there were no signs of structural collapse on the upper floor either. The hallways looked as solid as any other in the school, which is to say they listed slightly at odd angles but didn't look immediately hazardous. Nev's boots made hardly any sound against the floor's thick carpet of dust. There were other signs of invading animal life as well; long jagged scrapes across the ground and chunks torn or chewed from the wooden molding.

Nev paused to examine a large set of four gouges torn ragged and deep into a nearby wall. If they'd been made by claws, they were from something much bigger than a squirrel. Nev suddenly pictured a bear or a wolf getting in and went utterly still, trying to focus their hearing for sounds of larger animal life. Listening closely, Nev realized they could barely hear the voices of the other students just one floor below. A muffled murmur was all that made it through, punctuated by an occasional squeak from Beckett. No other sounds came, and after a moment, Nev continued down the hall. They had no desire to spend the rest of the night being assaulted by Victoria's scoffing.

The space was a perfect mirror of the students' dormitory tower, a place Nev was already becoming familiar with. The halls curved the same way, branching at the same points, flanked by door after door that led to small rooms with narrow beds. The familiar layout was made strange by dust and dark and silence. Nev stuck their head into some of the rooms as they passed. All had clearly gone unused for a long time, though many still bore the signs of their more lived-in days: open trunks with clothes strewn carelessly within, notes and photographs and drawings pinned to the wall or stacked on desks. On one desk was a small silver pocket watch, its ticking long silenced. Nev slipped it into their inner lower-left pocket, just in case.

It was all so strange. Nothing about the east wing matched with what Nev had heard about the accident that had supposedly taken place. Everything had simply been left there, sealed away for no reason that Nev could detect. It left Nev with an eerie feeling, as though the life that had inhabited this wing of the house had simply vanished, leaving an uncanny empty shell, waiting for something to come fill it up again.

Nev peered into several more rooms along the hall, each of them similar dormitory-style rooms to the one they lived in, each of them waiting for a return that wouldn't come. Nev's confusion deepened when they encountered a room with plates and bowls piled haphazardly in the center, like the remains of an abandoned picnic.

Nev was trying and failing to put the pieces of information together into some kind of understandable whole when they heard a noise. It was soft but startling in the silence, an uncertain *tap*. Nev whirled around, their candle guttering with the sudden movement. There was nothing in the hall behind them. The noise came again, from above. A searching, unsteady sound that slowly turned rhythmic, like steps.

Tak-a-tak-a-tak . . .

Nev stopped breathing. They strained their hearing, trying to pinpoint the exact location of the sound. It came from the next floor up, just above where Nev was standing. The clattering sound continued, steady and careful, moving closer.

"Nev—"

Nev yelped, whirling around in the other direction. This time their candle did go out, though the shadows were kept at bay by the light of the candle that Danny carried.

"Are you all right?" he asked.

"You know, for someone so big, you move very quietly," Nev said.

Danny grinned.

"I'm light on my feet."

"What are you doing here?" Nev asked. "Also, why do you have a sword?"

"It's a fencing foil," he said proudly. He rotated his hip to show the whiplike blade better in the candlelight. "I signed up to be on the team. I didn't know where Thaddeus was dragging me off to, and I wanted to be prepared."

Nev blinked.

"Deephaven has a fencing team?"

"This semester will mostly just be practice," Danny said, "but the first real match will be after the winter break. You should come."

He held out his candle to Nev while he talked, relighting theirs. He peered around the hall as the light increased, taking in the tomb-like atmosphere.

"Nev, please come back downstairs with me," he said. "It's not safe to be up here on your own."

"Isn't it?" Nev said. They shone their circle of candlelight around them. "Look. There is *no collapse*. Everyone just left their things here, but I don't see anything that would keep them from coming back. I don't understand why the wing is sealed up."

"Maybe it really *is* haunted," Danny said, a teasing tone to his voice.

Tak-a-tak-a-tak . . .

Nev and Danny's attention snapped in the same

64

direction, back down the curved hallway to where the stairway to the upper floor and lower floor met. Something moved down the stairway, slow and shuffling, a patch of black, its edges diluted by the surrounding darkness.

"Nev—" Danny whispered, moving to stand between Nev and the shape.

Tak-a-tak-a-tak . . .

It moved methodically, crouching low as it came down the stairs. It had a shuffling gait, slow and steady, a hunter not wishing to spook its prey.

The instant after they saw it, Nev could smell it. A burning iron stench, like hot metal or blood, hit them like a wall and seared the back of their throat. They gagged, stumbling back a few steps.

The dark shape, now at the bottom of the stairs, paused at Nev's sudden movement, considering them. Then it resumed its careful approach.

Tak-a-tak-a-tak . . .

It paused again at the edge of the first slice of dusty moonlight seeping in from the hallway windows. The pale light caught the edge of the thing's paw. It looked unnaturally elongated and covered in long, oily black hair that ran up its thin arms and seemed to cover its entire body. Long, strangely jointed fingers ended in curved black claws that clattered restlessly against the gouged floor, glinting from the faint reflection of Nev's and Danny's candles. The thing was silent, watching them from the mass of shadow and hair, its eyes two pale-fire pinpricks burning a cold blue.

It waited.

"Danny," Nev said, their voice less than a whisper.

Their chest felt too tight, unable to draw a proper breath, their tongue dry and heavy. Danny was staring straight ahead, unblinking, his hand on the hilt of his sword with a white-knuckle grip. Nev reached for his arm.

"Danny, don't—"

The shape shifted then, darkness coiling in on itself.

Just as quickly, it unwound, springing forward at a nightmare speed. As it scuttled toward them, in and out of the slivers of moonlight, Nev saw flickers of wide, staring eyes and a sinewy, wolflike shape. Its head was elongated, like a dog's muzzle, and large jagged teeth ran along the edges of a wide mouth.

TAK-A-TAK-A-TAK!

Danny moved first, jerking into sudden action. He seized Nev's arm in a vise grip, both of them dropping their candles uselessly on the floor as they ran, away from the stairs and the crooked thing that chased them.

TAK-A-TAK-A-TAK!

Nev found their feet, running alongside Danny. The two were guided only by the brief glimpses of moonlight, the memory of the similar space of the dormitory wing, and the animal sense screaming in the backs of their heads that they should keep as far away from the thing behind them as possible.

The hall opened up, branching into a corridor on the left and another flight of stairs leading up to the right. Without the slightest pause, Danny took the stairs, pulling Nev along with him. They hammered up the flight, taking the steps two at a time. The landing curved sharply to the left, and from the top Nev saw the shape scuttling low to the floor after them, its hairy limbs eating up the ground at a nightmare pace. It looked up as it came, its pale eyes burning into Nev's. It opened its jagged maw and screamed.

It was a horrible, high-pitched sound, and the burned-iron stench hit Nev like a physical blow. Danny retched, stumbling and falling to one knee. Nev stopped, pulling hard on Danny's arm, trying to haul him upright. "Come on!" Nev screamed. "Danny, it's—"

The beast unspooled from the stairway, lashing out a long arm. Danny whipped his fencing blade down to block it, but the flimsy blade caught on its claws and snapped. Danny stumbled backward as the beast reached for him. It snagged Danny's shoe, making him fall hard to the floor.

In an instant, the thing was on top of him. Long, stringy black hair dragged across his face as ragged claws scraped at his arms.

Another scream tore through the stillness, and for a terrible moment, Nev thought it was Danny's. But the beast pulled back, skittering away from the long silvery glint of Danny's sword. The sharp, broken point of it was coated in something black and wet. The disjointed shape of the beast hunched in on itself, giving a choking sob that Nev had heard before from the other side of the east wing door.

"Go!" Danny said breathlessly, scrabbling to his feet. "Run!"

The beast's sobs rose into a furious scream, and it lashed out again, its claws catching Danny in the side. The blow sent him sideways and he careened into the stairway banister. The ancient banister crumpled away from him with a brittle *crack*.

Danny fell, vanishing out of sight over the edge. An instant later there was a terrible crash of wood against stone, and a sharp, wet *snap*.

Then silence.

Nev pressed their hands to their mouth, too shocked to cry out. The beast stretched its neck out over the edge, its elongated maw framed by the moonlight, peering down at whatever disaster lay smashed below. Its head twisted around, the pale-fire eyes refocusing on Nev.

Nev ran.

They twisted left from the landing and into a short hallway. They didn't slow, didn't risk a single glance back at the terror right at their shoulder.

TAK-A-TAK-A-TAK!

The short hallway forked into a T shape, and Nev slid down the right-hand path. The clattering of the beast's claws was interrupted by a loud *whump* and the splintering of wood. It sounded as though the beast had tripped up trying to take the corner too quickly, though Nev didn't stop to look. They followed the curve of the hall, diving into the first open room they saw.

The hulking outlines of abandoned furniture loomed in the dark. Nev tucked behind a wardrobe and did their best to stop their heart from beating.

For a moment, for an eternity, Nev didn't hear anything. Even the self-conscious mumbling of the house had gone still. The silence stretched so long that Nev wondered if the beast had been gravely injured, or had simply given up, or had made its way back to Danny . . .

Tak-a-tak-a-tak . . .

Nev pressed as flat behind the wardrobe as possible.

Framed by the dim moonlight, the lank silhouette of the beast filled the doorway. The stench of blood and burned metal made Nev's eyes water, forcing them to clamp down on their own nose and mouth to keep from gagging. The beast swung its head low, back and forth, its long, oily hair dusting the ground as it searched.

It continued its shuffling way onward, all four of its disjointed limbs keeping it close to the ground, prowling. As it passed out of Nev's view, they saw spatters of a dark, wet substance trailing it on the ground from where Danny had wounded it.

Danny.

Nev waited as long as they dared, listening as that slow, steady *tak-a-tak* faded down the hallway. Nev took a long, steadying breath, then another. They crept out from the shadows, heading toward Danny and away from the beast.

At the base of the stairs was a pile of dry, splintered wood that had once been a banister, and nestled in the middle of it like a bird in its nest was Danny's crumpled body. Nev didn't want to go near the pile, didn't want to see, but they knew they had to. They crept silently to him, keeping an ear out for the clattering of the beast's claws above. They pulled Danny gingerly by the shoulder and turned him over.

He groaned loudly. Nev had to suppress the urge to smother the sound with their hands even as relief flooded through them. They turned their head back toward the stairs. Still no sign or sound of the beast.

Danny was ashen and sweating, clutching his left arm to his chest. His breathing came ragged.

"Danny?" Nev whispered.

"My arm," Danny croaked. "I think I broke my arm."

"It's all right," Nev said, though they both knew that wasn't true. "Danny, we have to get out of here before it comes back. Can you stand?"

"I-I think so . . ." Danny struggled into a sitting position, his face screwed up in concentration and pain. Nev slung his good arm around their shoulders, helping him the rest of the way to his feet. Nev listened again. Still silence, though it had a different quality to it now; the feeling of something listening back.

"Come on, we have to leave," Nev said. They crouched down quickly to pick up Danny's broken sword from the rubble. "If we head back, join the others—"

Tak-a-tak-a-tak . . .

"Let's go!" The sound was too close, moving too fast. Nev stumbled down the nearest hallway, one hand supporting Danny and the other gripping the fencing foil. Danny gasped in pain at the rapid movement. Nev could feel his sweat soaking through his pajamas.

"Nev," he gasped, "we can't go back down there. The others—The door is locked, they—we're helpless."

Nev cursed. Danny was right; going back downstairs would be making all of them easy prey. They continued to drag Danny down the hallway, their mechanical mind wheeling through their options.

"There has to be another way out of the east wing," Nev muttered. Their mind turned back to the dormitory wing, the still-living twin to the empty tower, trying to sort through all its little doors and passageways. Then it came to them.

"The service lift," they said.

Nev dragged Danny a few more doors down the hallway, throwing one open to reveal not a room, but a shallow closet. Among the abandoned brooms and buckets was another, smaller door. They pulled

Danny into the room, talking low in an attempt to keep both of them calm.

"In our dormitory, this leads to the laundry wash-room," they said.

"W-where does this one lead?" Danny stammered through clenched teeth.

"Away from here."

Nev propped Danny against some nearby shelves and wrestled the small lift door open. The square metal lift inside was shallow, perhaps just big enough to fit two frightened students.

"Climb in," Nev said.

"What?" Danny's eyes went wide in his pain-stricken face. "I-I can't."

"Come on, that thing is coming!"

Nev searched around the edge of the lift in the dark, until their fingers brushed against a small lever. With any luck, the lift would provide a way out of the wing. Then they and Danny could go get help.

"Please," Danny said. "Nev, I can't. It's too small."

Tak-a-tak-a-tak . . .

Nev moved so that Danny was trapped between them and the lift.

"I'm sorry, Danny," Nev said. "It'll only be for a moment."

They shoved Danny into the lift, throwing their

whole body against him. The much larger boy stiffened, instinctively struggling. But he was tired and injured and scared. He allowed himself to be crammed into the lift, curling in on himself as his shoulders shook. His breath came out in little panicked gasps as Nev folded into the lift beside them. They could still hear the clatter of the beast's claws, but they couldn't see it yet. Nev reached out and pulled the service lift's lever.

The lift shuddered once and fell still. They didn't move.

"Nev?" Danny said, his voice like a fiddle string about to snap. "I can't be in here. I can't be in small spaces."

Nev closed the door of the lift as much as they could to hide them from outside view.

"I can fix it," they said. "I just need to get to the pulley system."

They felt quickly around the lift's metal interior, searching for a seam. They found it easily enough, a small maintenance hatch just above their head. Nev pried it open, gazing into the ravenous black within. They shoved their hand in blindly, feeling for the lift's mechanism.

"Nev, *please*."

At first, all they felt was dust and cobwebs. Then

their fingers collided with something solid: a pulley. A thick cable wound around its edge. Nev followed the cable with their fingers to another gear, which led to another, which led to—

Nothing.

An empty space where a wheel should be, the missing piece likely long fallen to the lift's shaft. Nev withdrew their hand from the hatch. They rummaged quickly through their coat's many pockets, searching for anything that might be of use. The clockwork gears were too small, but maybe something else . . .

"I have to get out," Danny choked. "Nev, I have to *get out.*"

He began to struggle. Nev braced their body against the walls of the lift, blocking his exit.

"Almost there, we're almost there," Nev said, trying to keep their voice even and soothing. "I know how to fix it, I just need—"

From their inner upper-right pocket, Nev pulled a gleaming silvery wheel: the large bobbin.

"This."

They reached back up into the hatch, wedging in both hands as best they could into the small gap. They found the missing space again, pulling down hard on the cord with one hand and slotting the bobbin into place with the other. They fumbled with the heavy cord, trying to slide it into the grooves of the bobbin.

Out of the corner of their eye, they noticed a shift of the darkness and turned to see the pale-fire eyes of the beast staring through the gap in the lift door, inches from Nev's face.

The whites of its eyes were visible all around the frigid blue gleam as its gaze caught Nev and held them fast.

The cord slid into place, and with a terrific shriek, the lift suddenly plummeted downward into the dark.

The air was snatched out of Nev's lungs, and so they were silent as the house swallowed them up, the beast's burning eyes watching as they and Danny fell.

Chapter Six

Nev stood in the dark, back in that tiny hallway in the tiny apartment. Serious men in dark suits crowded around, pushing past them. They weren't there for Nev. They dragged Nev's father from the front room, where he'd fallen asleep on the couch again. He was pulled along, bleary-eyed and confused, out of the apartment. He reached back with a look of desperation growing on his face.

"Guinevere, please."

Nev didn't move. They felt as though their feet had sunk into the musty carpet. This had happened before, but it was different now, and both Nev and their father could feel it. This couldn't go on. Something had to change.

"Nev, *please!*"

❧

"Nev, *please!*"

Nev jerked awake from their nightmare with the dim awareness of something shifting beneath them. For a terrible moment they thought they'd gone blind; eyes opened or closed didn't make a difference. The world around them was just inky blackness, and everything hurt.

The thing beneath them moved again, struggling weakly.

"Nev . . ." Danny groaned.

Nev scrabbled off of him as quickly as they could, colliding with something heavy and wooden. Their limbs felt numb and tingly, jarred from the fall. They felt around blindly in the dark, trying to get their bearings but afraid of what they might touch. They felt twisted metal and splintered wood: the remains of the service lift. They must have fallen to the bottom of the shaft.

"Danny? Are you all right?"

"No," Danny croaked in reply, but his voice sounded relieved through the pain.

79

Nev shuffled on their hands and knees in the direction of his voice. They eventually found the edge of his shoe among the wreckage.

"I'm sorry," Nev said. "I couldn't think of what else to do."

"It's all right," came Danny's voice. "It's better than being eaten, I suppose."

Nev looked up toward where they thought the service lift shaft would be, trying to see where they had fallen from. They thought they saw a tiny pin-prick of light, high above, though it could have just been their eyes trying to make sense of the velvet void that surrounded them.

"Nev? What *was* that thing?"

"I-I don't know," they whispered, and they didn't want to think about it while sitting in the dark. They rummaged in their coat pockets, bringing out the box of matches. They'd lost the candles somewhere above, but a little light was better than none.

It took a couple of tries to strike a match in total darkness, and when it caught, Nev had to squint against the sudden flare. Danny lay nearby, curled around his injured arm among the wreckage of the lift. The square opening of the shaft was directly above them. Around them was what looked like a small room, though Nev couldn't actually see any of its walls in the dark. Crowded around the two huddled students were boxes and barrels and tall shelves laden with a variety of objects, only the edges of which were picked out by the dimming light.

The match burned out. Nev struck another.

"Are we in the basement?" Danny said.

"We must be," Nev said, though it didn't look like the sort of basement that belonged to a school. It would have been better suited as storage for a museum. Instead of things like spare desks or notebooks, there were dusty jars and straw-packed boxes, filled with carved wooden icons, masks, ornate and ancient-looking books and scrolls. Framed paintings and etchings leaned in stacks against the towering shelves, partially wrapped in paper or cloth. Small cardstock tags were attached to many of the items with string, an indecipherable scrawl labeling them. The air was dry, and there was a slight acrid, burning smell that Nev didn't want to think too much about. They lit another match as the one between their fingers burned out.

Danny pulled himself up stiffly, laying his broken fencing foil in his lap. The whiplike blade was bent, the sharp, broken edge still coated in a black, dried substance.

"I think I injured it," Danny said.

"If you bring those reflexes to your fencing matches, you'll be the team captain in no time," Nev replied.

Danny blinked up at them. His stunned expression slid sideways into a lopsided grin, and he began to laugh. So did Nev. It felt strangely involuntary, the laughter forcing its way out in harsh gasps. Nev wondered if this was what being hysterical felt like.

The laughter subsided, and the tomb silence of the basement reasserted itself.

"Nev," Danny said quietly, fear creeping back into his voice, "seriously, what *was* that thing? Some kind of wolf, or a bear?"

"I don't know," Nev said, but they were certain that whatever it was, it wasn't a wolf or a bear. It wasn't *natural*. They could tell from Danny's expression that he was thinking the same thing.

"What's it *doing* here in the house?" Danny went on. "Oh God, the others! They're still locked in with that thing!"

The panic was infectious, tightening its fist around Nev's chest. They shoved their hands deep into their pockets, taking a steadying breath. This was a problem like any other. Mechanical. Solvable. All they had to do was determine the order of operations. First things first.

"Let's focus on getting out of here," Nev said. "Then we can go help the others."

Danny cursed painfully under his breath as he hauled himself out of the lift's wreckage, using the ruined sword to prop himself up. Nev struck another match, holding it up high as they squeezed between the overstuffed racks. They scanned the darkened edges of the room, looking for a door, but their eyes kept snagging on the curios piled around them. Their fingers itched to pick up a small, hammered silver ring resting in the middle of a nest of crumpled green velvet. There was a shape cut out of the band, a rough silhouette of a person. Nev went to reach for it but stopped themself. Focus. They didn't know what this place was. Its strangeness, its familiar burned-metal smell, unnerved them.

"What *is* all this?" Nev muttered.

"I get the feeling we're not supposed to know about this place," Danny said.

He slid along the other side of the shelf, and Nev could hear rustling as he sifted through the artifacts.

Nev held the match closer to the shelf next to them. Everything looked carefully organized, though nearly all of it was covered in a thick layer of dust. They picked up a framed etching, the image done in dark, heavy lines. It showed a lonely stone chapel, nestled among the steep forested hills around it. The feeling of familiarity nagged at Nev, before they realized they were looking at an image of what Deephaven Academy used to be, before the wings of the house had been built around the small church at its heart. It made them feel strange to look at the image, like looking at the skeleton of someone they knew.

They put the etching hurriedly back on the shelf, their fingers leaving streaks through the dust clouding the frame's protective glass. In the same motion, Nev's hand brushed against the soft leather cover of a small black notebook. They pulled it from the shelf and flipped open the cover, trying to stifle a sneeze at the musty smell that rose up from the yellowing pages.

The book seemed to be a journal, handwritten with a looping scrawl in faded brown ink. The words were in a language Nev couldn't read and didn't recognize. There were also inscrutable hand-drawn diagrams, anatomical drawings, and circular charts. Something about the scribbly way the drawings were done, the way the writing had a haphazard intensity to it, made Nev think that it had been written by someone close to their age, perhaps another student.

Nev peered back up at the shelves. None of the pieces fit together; some of the artifacts were clearly handmade: clusters of sticks bound with ornate tangles of twine, uncanny cloth dolls with roughly stitched likenesses. Other objects looked more refined, older. Heavy books with ornate embellishments on their leather spines, or complex metal instruments and puzzle boxes.

"I think this stuff was confiscated from students," Nev said, "or it's kept down here to make sure we don't fiddle with it. These things feel . . . out of place. Wrong, somehow, like—"

"Like the thing up in the east wing," Danny said.

Nev nodded, remembering the terrible, cold stare of the thing, and shuddered.

Nev looked back down at the journal and wondered what the densely packed writing might say, what it might tell them. They slid the journal into their outer lower-right pocket. Just this one thing, then. Just in case.

There was a loud thump from the other side of the shelf, startling Nev, followed by more cursing from Danny.

"Are you all right?" Nev said.

"Mostly," Danny said. "I think I found a way out."

Nev stepped carefully around the shelf of artifacts to where Danny was standing, the dim light from their match barely picking out the edges of a stepladder. Nev lit another match, revealing a closed hatch above them. Danny had climbed up the steps and was pushing against the hatch with his uninjured arm. The hatch stayed shut.

"Hang on," Danny said. "It's not locked. It feels like there's something on top of it."

He climbed up a couple more steps, bracing his broad shoulders against the hatch. He pushed and almost lost his footing as the smooth soles of his leather shoes slid in the thick dust.

With a deep grunt, Danny heaved again and the hatch swung out and open, a heavy crash accompanying it as whatever had rested on it was sent toppling. Nev and Danny froze at the clamor. They didn't know how the room might connect to the east wing, who or what the noise might have alerted.

Danny gripped the hilt of his ruined fencing foil and carefully peered over the lip of the hatch.

"It's all right," Danny said, and he climbed awkwardly out, cradling his injured arm to his chest. Nev followed quickly after.

They found themselves, confusingly, in another basement. A proper one this time, filled with jars of food preserves and tins of seasoning and flour. A small window near the ceiling let in a sliver of moonlight, illuminating a small stairway and a door into the house proper.

Danny glanced back at the yawning black portal they'd just come through.

"An under-basement?"

"The house seems to have more than a few secrets," Nev said.

Nev closed the hatch and, with Danny's help, righted the fallen crate of potatoes and slid it back over the top. They had a feeling that Principal Blanchly would not be forgiving about their clambering around a hidden subbasement.

Still, Nev made a careful mental note of what the crate looked like and its position. They were going to want to get a closer look at the contents hidden below, sooner or later.

Nev and Danny exited out of the basement and into the house's impressive and empty kitchens, and from there out into the familiar dining room. They moved as quickly and as quietly as they could, following the twisted halls back around to the bell-strung door of the east wing. The bells hung limp from their rope, and the padlock on the door was firmly in place. There was no sign of Thaddeus.

Nev stopped before the door and listened, holding their breath.

"I don't hear anything," Danny whispered.

"That's either a good sign or a very bad one," Nev said.

They hefted the heavy padlock in their hand. Nev had figured out how to pick locks from a young age, just another machine they'd learned to take apart and put back together as needed. They rummaged through their coat's many pockets, looking for something that would serve as a suitable pick.

"Here," Danny said, offering his broken fencing foil.

Nev took the blade with a grateful nod, trying to ignore the dark stain that still covered the tip. They inserted the flexible metal into the padlock's keyhole, and after a moment of feeling their way through the inner mechanisms, the lock sprung open with a satisfying *thunk*.

They handed the blade back to Danny, the broken tip now bent horribly. Danny sighed at the damage but readied his grip on the sword. He nodded once to Nev.

Nev nodded and pulled back the bolt, braced for whatever might be waiting inside, and threw open the door.

They were met with a startled yelp from Beckett. The three other first-year students stood around the campfire of candles, staring wide-eyed at the unexpected movement from the door. They all looked surprised, even Victoria, though her expression shifted to haughty irritation when she saw who it was.

There was no sign of the beast.

"How did *you* get out *there*?" Beckett asked, accusation mixing with the fear on his face, as though Nev and Danny's sudden reappearance gave them away as the rumored ghosts of the east wing.

"What happened to your arm?" Agnes said, angling her head at Danny's injury.

"It'll be fine," Danny said, though he still winced. "Is everyone all right?"

"Of course," Victoria said acidly. "*We* aren't the ones who went wandering off into a condemned part of the house."

"We thought you'd died," Agnes said, matter-of-factly. "We heard some yelling and a crash. We were going to check on you."

"I wasn't," Victoria said.

"We decided it was safer to just wait," Beckett said.

"Well, we're fine," Nev said. Their eyes kept scanning the winding stairway, looking for any movement in the darkness. "But we have to leave, now."

Beckett looked conflicted.

"But Thaddeus said—"

"Thaddeus isn't here," Danny said. "Come on, it isn't safe."

"No argument from me," Victoria said.

She drew her robe more tightly around her nightshirt and strode out between Nev and Danny, heading toward the dormitory wing without a backward glance. Beckett scurried out after her as if the east wing were on fire, and Agnes took a moment to blow out all of the candles so it wouldn't be.

"We should tell the principal," Beckett squeaked. "We could have been seriously hurt in there."

"No," Nev said, suddenly and forcefully. Danny's eyebrows shot up at this.

"No," Nev continued, more gently. "It won't help anything. Thaddeus is a prefect; it's his word against ours. We'd only get in trouble."

Beckett nodded hesitantly. He grabbed an extra candle from Agnes, and together they headed back to the dormitories. With one more glance at the still room, Nev shut the door and latched it. They replaced the lock, clicking it shut with extra force, as though that would help to contain the thing that waited inside.

They strung the bells back across the door, taking care to not let any of them ring, and paused. They didn't know what the purpose of those bells were.

Now they wondered if they were meant to alert someone of anything trying to get out of the east wing.

"Nev, are we really not going to tell the principal about what we saw in there?"

Danny was frowning down at them. Nev stared at the dark wood of the east wing door and the thick bell-strung rope across it.

"That thing is hiding in the east wing," Nev said, "and somebody hid it there."

Danny was quiet for a moment as he took in their words. "And you think that someone is Principal Blanchly," he said.

"Maybe. I can't see how she wouldn't know about it, at least, and I don't know why she would keep it a secret," Nev said. "I don't know. But I don't think we should say anything yet, not until I find out more."

"Nev, that thing almost *killed us*," Danny said. "We can't just stay here and—"

"I know," Nev said. "But I don't have anywhere else I can go."

Danny gave them another long look before sighing wearily.

"No, I suppose I don't either," he said.

"We *do* need to get your arm fixed, though," Nev said. "Come on, I'll walk with you to Professor Tieran's room."

Tieran, in addition to teaching biology and mathematics, acted as the academy's nurse. Nev thought Danny's arm looked bad enough that he might need to be driven into town to get it set properly.

"I can go myself," Danny said. "You go back to bed. There will be more questions if we turn up together."

"What will you say happened?"

Danny shrugged. "I'll come up with something. Maybe I tripped down the stairs while headed to the toilet. She'd probably believe that."

They walked together back to the main hall before Danny split off to the wing where the teachers lived during the semester. He paused to cast a concerned backward glance at Nev before the house carried him from view.

Nev picked their way back to their room, closing the door and locking it tightly. In every dark corner, they thought they saw glimpses of two pale-fire pinpricks staring out at them. Nev pulled several candles from the desk drawer, filling the small bedroom with as much warm light as they could. They curled up on the narrow bed, the comforting weight of their coat still around their shoulders.

Nev didn't sleep that night.

Around them, the house turned over and groaned, just as restless.

Chapter Seven

Despite the terror of the night before, the sun still rose over Deephaven Academy, bringing with it the first day of classes. Nev was caught up in a dreamlike sense of normalcy. They got up with the sun, having not slept at all, dressed for the day, and joined the flow of students down to the dining hall for breakfast.

Nev didn't see Danny at all that morning. They passed the other first-year students at the absurdly full breakfast table, but they all avoided Nev and each other, pointedly not making eye contact. They each seemed to want to put the previous night's misadventure out of their minds, which was fine as far as Nev was concerned. They couldn't risk Principal Blanchly hearing about it. At best, they'd be expelled for romping around in the forbidden wing of the house. At worst, they'd run afoul of whatever secrets the principal might be hiding. Either way, Nev thought it was best to go unnoticed, a responsible model student, at least until they knew exactly what they were up against.

Nev sat alone at a little table, tucked in the corner and out of the way. They looked out at the bustling sea of students, wondering how any of them could laugh and joke and gossip, all while some terrible, ravenous thing lurked nearby, with only a few hallways, a locked door, and a string of bells between them. Did they all really not know about it?

Nev alternated between taking half-hearted bites of their buttered toast and fiddling with their latest project: a clockwork rabbit that would jump into the air when wound up. As they fit the gears together, they felt their anxiety calm a little. It helped, when they were distracted or worried, to have something for their hands to do. It felt good to be able to put something together, to know how something was intended to work and know that, with a little resourcefulness, it could be fixed. Anything could be fixed.

If only the world around them worked the same way.

Nev's first class was Innovations in Biology with Professor Tieran, a short woman, barely taller than Nev, with long, frizzy red hair that had prominent gray streaks running from her temples. She wore a loose, comfortable-looking cardigan over her blouse. She smiled warmly at her small class of students as they filed into the room, still chatting amiably after breakfast.

It had been a couple of years since Nev had attended school, having had to drop out to take care of their father. Even without recent experience they knew the way Deephaven arranged its classes was odd. The house didn't have proper classrooms. Instead, small groups of students organized roughly by age would gather in various sitting rooms, settling into a mismatched collection of armchairs and cushions covered in old velvet. The seats were placed in a loose half-moon shape, facing the instructor.

Nev sank into an ancient purple armchair and pulled out a small notebook and a fountain pen from their inner upper-left pocket. Professor Tieran strode up to the large chalkboard set along one wall, the slate painted a checkerboard pattern from the gold late-morning light streaming in through the lattice windows.

"Good morning, friends," she said, a pleasant rasp to her voice. "I'm glad to see that you're all feeling enthusiastic. I see a few familiar faces here, and a few new ones. I won't make you introduce yourselves now, I know how intimidating a new school can be, but I hope to get to know each of you better as your time at Deephaven goes on."

Her eyes lingered on each student as she spoke. When her attention reached Nev, they felt the warmth of her kind regard. It was so different from Principal Blanchly's steely nature that it felt almost startling.

"Now, we've got the whole mystery of existence to unravel, so we'd best get started."

She turned and began to sketch out the beginnings of an anatomical diagram, when everyone's attention was diverted by the sound of the door creaking open. Danny stood in the doorway, looking sheepish. His left arm hung from a sling, held close to his chest, with a messy stack of papers under his other arm.

"Mr. Harper," Tieran said with that same warm smile. "Glad to have you back. I see the doctor was able to patch you up from your little accident last night."

"Yes, ma'am," Danny said. He spotted Nev and hurriedly pushed a nearby chair next to them, its legs squeaking in protest across the wood floor. Professor

Tieran winced at the sound before turning back to the blackboard.

"Now, I thought it would be prudent to begin our study of biology with a look at our own. We are a fascinating machine, full of glorious contradictions and carefully balanced mechanisms."

She continued on, sketching out an impressively detailed diagram of a human muscular system. Nev tried to keep up, following the sketch in their notebook, but their attention was disrupted by the sound of low, frantic rustling. They looked over to see Danny struggling with his one good hand in his pockets while his stack of note-taking paper balanced precariously on his knee. Nev drew a spare fountain pen out of their inner upper-right pocket, passing it wordlessly to Danny. He accepted it with a grateful smile.

Nev found their eyes lingering on his injured arm, and for a moment they were back in the east wing, the terrible long limbs of the beast reaching toward them, its eyes burning hungrily in the dark.

Nev turned back toward the professor and buried the memories in the complex lesson.

The end of class was signaled by a low chime from a dark-wood grandfather clock, which stood in one corner of the room. Nev was finishing off a final scrawl of notes when Danny leaned over, handing back their spare pen.

"Thanks," he said.

Nev nodded. "How's your arm?"

Danny shrugged and immediately winced in pain at the motion.

"Nev, can we talk about—"

"Mr. Harper, would you mind staying behind a moment?" Professor Tieran said. She smiled at him, pity glittering in her eyes. "I'd like to check the doctor's work on that arm of yours. Not that I don't trust his expertise."

"Of course, Professor," Danny said, returning her smile. He glanced at Nev.

"I'll catch up with you later?"

Nev nodded again, slipped their notebook and pens into their pocket, and hurried out.

They didn't quite know what to make of Danny. Most of the students at Deephaven preferred to keep to themselves, including Nev. Even Patience seemed to have her own group of regular admirers that she kept to. Danny, however, seemed determined to try to make friends with everyone. And yet, there had been that moment the night before, when Victoria had brought up Danny's father and his eyes had gone cold.

There was a lot Nev had to learn about the people they were now living with.

Of course, the most pressing puzzle in Nev's mind was of the thing locked in the east wing, what it was doing there, and why. Clearly someone knew the beast was there and wasn't concerned for the safety of the school. Maybe the lock on the door was enough. Maybe the beast would find its own way out eventually and escape into the surrounding woods, no longer a danger to the students. Maybe Nev could just forget about it and carry on with building their new life.

Nev wasn't that kind of person.

So, with some time until their next class, Nev went to the only place they knew to get answers: the library.

❧

Deephaven's library was in a massive room built along the south-facing side of the academy. It was two stories tall, the second floor overlooking the first through a long cutout in the floor. Tall windows lined one side of the space, filling it with all the light the valley could provide.

Rows and rows of dark-wood bookshelves held everything from obscure social treaties to evolutionary theory to novels. Small tables and chairs were tucked into every available corner, providing privacy and quiet to read and study.

Nev passed by several other students tucked into corners and frowning at piles of open books, notebooks balanced on their knees, already busy this early in the term. They made their way to the librarian's desk, a sprawling surface placed near the window that got the most light and had the best view of the valley. The librarian was a tall person with wavy dark brown hair and brassy wire-rimmed spectacles. They were wearing a cream linen suit with the clips of various fountain pens showing from their breast pocket. Their attention was entirely absorbed in a slim paperback novel.

"Excuse me," Nev said, with the hushed tone that all libraries seemed to demand.

After a silent moment, the librarian turned their head slowly toward Nev, though their eyes continued to track the words on the page for a moment longer.

"Hmm?" the librarian said.

"I was wondering if there are recent records from the area kept here," Nev said. "Newspapers, that sort of thing."

The librarian sat silent, staring at Nev in a way that felt as if they weren't really looking *at* them, but somehow beyond. Then they blinked, shaking slightly.

"Oh yes," the librarian said. "We have a lot of that sort of thing. Newspapers, obituaries, historical writings. Mostly from the nearby town, you understand, though there is a small subsection on Deephaven and the ecology of the surrounding woods. Was there anything specific you were looking for?"

"No," Nev said, though that wasn't true. They just didn't think "has a long-haired monster been seen stalking the area, and what is it?" would yield results. "I just want to learn more about the area. I'm new here."

The librarian nodded absently, tucked the battered paperback into the large pocket of their jacket, and walked out into the shelves. Nev, assuming they were meant to follow, trailed after.

The librarian moved slowly, but their long legs seemed to eat up the ground beneath them, and soon Nev lost sight of them in the stacks. It was only when the librarian gave a polite clearing of their throat that Nev found them again between two towering shelves, pulling down stacks of folios. They placed them down in a neat pile on a nearby study table.

"These go back for the past five years," the librarian said. "If you want a more comprehensive local history, come fetch me at the desk and I'll dig around in the archives for you."

"Thank you," Nev said, but the tall librarian was already drifting back to their desk, the battered paperback open again in their hand.

Nev sat in the lone, high-backed chair by the small table, untied the ribbon holding the cardboard folio closed, and began reading.

They scanned the headlines of the nearby town's small monthly newspapers, looking for stories about strange animal attacks, or sightings in the woods, or anything having to do with Deephaven. There was a series of columns that ran for nearly a year tracking the whereabouts of an ornery badger that harassed the township, complete with a particularly angry-looking illustration, though Nev didn't think it was relevant. There were nature guides and bird-watching annotations, but nothing about a violent, blue-eyed beast.

As far as mentions of Deephaven itself, there were surprisingly few. Occasionally, there would be features on one of the academy's prominent alumni, detailing a recent scientific breakthrough or a celebrated novel. In these features, Deephaven itself was hardly mentioned, much of it simply describing the alumni as having been "educated in the area."

Then Nev came across an article dated earlier that year: a report on the tragic death of Naomi Wharton, the daughter of an aristocratic family from the United

Kingdom and a student at "the nearby academy." The article didn't talk much about Naomi herself, only that she had died due to a "structural incident" at the academy. As of the writing of the article, her body had not yet been recovered, and the principal was organizing a search of the accident site.

So it was true; a student *had* died in the east wing. But the cause of death couldn't have been any kind of "structural incident." Nev had seen the place, whole and intact. The only reason Nev could think the principal had lied to the local reporter, to the girl's family even, was if the truth was more strange and terrible. The poor girl must have been killed by the beast. But why was it still in the house all those months later?

Nev searched through more newspapers but got no further insight. They let out a frustrated sigh. They stacked the newspaper folios in a neat pile for the librarian to reshelve and stretched, sending a loud *pop* echoing through the quiet space. They needed some fresh air to think.

Though Deephaven was surrounded by the thick tangle of the woods and the steep slopes of the surrounding valley hills, the grounds immediately around the school were well maintained to give space for students to stretch their legs. A path of large flat stones circled the towers of the academy, with low hedges to mark the boundary of the school grounds and the forest proper. There was the driveway at the front, leading out into the valley, and behind the house was a long field. On warm days, the field played host to students reading in the sun and, Nev assumed, the occasional fencing practice.

They tucked their hands into their pockets to shield them from the chilly autumn breeze as they walked, and felt their fingers bump up against an unfamiliar object. They pulled out the small leather-bound journal they had found in the basement the night before. They flipped it open, hoping for some revelation in the full light of day.

The unfamiliar language of the notebook was just as unreadable as it had been the night before. Nev paged through, trying to find some mark of owner-ship. Nothing, though they saw that a small section of the book's pages was missing. It looked as though someone had taken a fistful of pages and torn them from the spine. Thinking back to their time in the hidden under-basement, Nev didn't remember seeing any loose pages scattered around. Their first thought was that someone was trying to hide some secret written in the journal, but why bother when the lan-guage couldn't be read anyway? Did it have anything to do with what was hidden in the east wing, or was it unrelated, just another riddle?

Nev closed the notebook and pocketed it with a sigh. The secrets hidden within Deephaven's walls were unnatural, unsettling, *dangerous*. Someone was keeping those secrets hidden from the world, and until Nev knew exactly who or why, the danger would not stay confined to the east wing for long.

Nev didn't mean to end up on the grounds in front of the east wing's tower, but soon enough they found themself staring up at its facade. The windows were blue mirrors, reflecting the clear autumn sky. The fact that Nev couldn't see into them was an unexpected relief. They weren't ready to face the thing that hid there again.

Nev wondered if it slept during the day, if it slept at all. They wondered if it was up in the tower, right now, gazing down at them with its pale-fire eyes.

Nev shuddered, terrified at the thought, and quickly turned away, bumping squarely into Danny's chest.

"Danny!" Nev startled. "You've got to make a noise or something before coming up on people."

"Sorry," Danny said cheerily.

He looked well recovered from the previous night's terror, despite his sling-wrapped arm. He had on a fresh button-up shirt and dark slacks with a matching vest. Though his lopsided smile was firmly back in place, Nev noticed that he was studiously avoiding looking at the exterior of the east wing.

"What did Professor Tieran say?" they asked.

"She said it will take a little while to heal. She set the bone last night and had me driven to the doctor in town this morning. Oh, and she warned me that when I go to the bathroom in the dark, I should take a candle."

Nev nodded, relieved. Out of the corner of their eye, they thought they saw something move in one of the upper floors of the tower. They looked up and saw nothing but the same still-glass mirror of the sky.

"What are we going to do?" Danny said.

He was looking at them, having seen their gaze shift to the windows of the wing.

Nev shook their head. "I have to find out who brought that thing into the house, and I need to find out how to get rid of it."

"Don't take this the wrong way," Danny said carefully, "but why don't *you* leave?"

Nev blinked at him.

"What?"

"Not that I want you to," Danny said quickly. "Sorry, that didn't come out right. But Nev, what we saw in there, it wasn't *natural*. There's something really weird going on at the academy. It's not safe here. You don't have to stay."

"I *do* have to," Nev said. "It's complicated. Deephaven is as close to a home as I have right now. I can't go back."

Danny was silent, waiting. Nev sighed.

"My mom left, a long time ago. I don't know where she went, or where she is, because she didn't see fit to tell me or my father. My father didn't handle it well, and then things got bad. Things got bad for almost everyone back then, I guess, but they've stayed bad for a long time for him. He—well, he tried some bad ideas, hoping to help make life better, but it didn't and he didn't really try very hard. He got in trouble with people you shouldn't get in trouble with, and now he's not in a position to help anyone."

Danny looked stricken.

"Nev, I-I'm sorry, I had no idea—"

"He's not *dead*, Danny. He just got arrested. Anyway, what about you?" Nev said, eager to shift the focus off of themself. "You're the one who got hurt. Why don't *you* go home?"

Danny snorted. "Because Victoria was right about what she said about my dad last night. He's terrible. If it's a choice between being locked up here or locked up in his house, I'll pick here. At least there are other people to talk to."

"You were locked up?" Nev said.

Danny gave another shrug and another wince.

"Might as well have been. My parents only dragged me out of the house when there was enough of a public outcry over them tearing down homes to make room for my dad's 'little investments.' After all, the great Mr. Harper can't be a heartless slumlord if his own son was adopted from the very streets he's paving, can he?"

Bitterness dripped from Danny's every word, so much so that it made Nev flinch. Danny gazed steadily up at the east wing tower now, avoiding Nev's eye.

"I'm just a useful shield for him," Danny continued, "except for when I'm not. One of his investor buddies told him about an out-of-the-way private school where I could be stashed when I'm *inconvenient*. My father jumped at the idea."

"Danny, I . . . I don't know what to say," Nev said. They were never very good at conversations, especially the serious ones. Were they supposed to hug him?

"You don't have to say anything," Danny said, flashing that lopsided smile, the venom melting away from his voice. "Personally, I thought being sent here was the best thing he'd ever done for me. I'd get to try out for sports teams, talk to people who aren't always trying to sell something. I could finally make some friends."

He smiled at Nev again. They shifted uncomfortably. They *really* weren't good at this kind of conversation.

"But then you learned what else is locked up here with us," they said.

Danny nodded.

"Well, once we find out what the beast is and how to get rid of it, maybe it'll be a decent place after all."

Nev startled at his use of *we*.

"Danny, you're hurt. You could have *died*. I can do this on my own."

"Maybe, but you won't have to," Danny replied. "If you're going to face an actual monster, you'll need someone who can swing a sword."

Nev wanted to protest, wanted to tell Danny that they could do it alone, that no one else's life would be ruined because of them. Not again. But they were tired, and scared, and if they were honest, lonely too.

"*Can* you still swing a sword?" was all they said, nodding to Danny's injured arm.

"The team captain was *not* thrilled," Danny said. "I'm lucky I only hurt my off hand. I just hope I'm all healed up in time for the first proper match."

"Well, maybe we'll get eaten by then and it won't be a problem," Nev said, and winced at their own misguided attempt at a joke.

They really, *really* weren't good at conversations.

Danny smiled anyway. Nev noticed that he seemed to take any opportunity he could to smile.

"I'm glad that's settled," he said. "We'll just have to do our best not to be eaten."

Nev turned back toward the house's entrance with Danny beside them. As they did, movement from the east wing caught their eye again, snapping their attention back to its looming face. They studied it, then let their eyes lose focus, fuzzing the details of the house and searching only for the movement.

They found it.

"Nev? What is it?"

Nev pointed up at the third floor of the east wing's tower.

"Look."

For another moment, all was still. Then a slight shift of the breeze curled its way through the valley, causing one of the narrow lattice windows to swing gently back and forth, kept slightly open by some small object wedged in its sill.

Someone had been sneaking into the east wing from the outside, and they'd kept their path open.

Chapter Eight

The steady cycle of classes kept moving onward, weeks of rambling lectures and late-night study sessions, and soon Nev fell into a comfortable routine. Every morning, they would wake from the now-familiar nightmares of long ragged limbs and gleaming blue eyes, get dressed and slip into their jacket, and head off to breakfast. Sometimes Danny would join them, sometimes he was at fencing practice. Nev would be attentive in their classes, taking notes and working hard, doing their best impression of a model student. Nev found it amazing how quickly they got used to the strange rhythms of Deephaven. It was almost enough to let them believe the source of their nightmares was nothing more than their own anxious imagination, brought on by the stress of starting at a new school, a new life. Almost, but not quite.

Even as the daily routine asserted itself, Nev kept an eye out for something that didn't fit, the thread to pull that might unravel the mystery of the east wing.

They finally found it in Professor Bellairs's class.

A Study of Languages was held in the square, cozy room that the professor had claimed to host his lectures. The walls were made up of inset shelves, holding everything from ancient-looking hand-bound manuscripts to relatively modern language textbooks. Bellairs himself sat between two imposing shelves, the wall behind him above the wood risers painted chalkboard black, with Latin conjugations scrawled upon it in neat rows.

Professor Bellairs had sunk into an ancient purple-velvet armchair, his fingers laced in a steeple in front of him, his head leaned back and his eyes half-closed as he spoke. He was dressed in a warm yellow tweed suit, and a gentle smile was set upon his round face.

"Latin," he was saying, "isn't properly a dead language, like many today would wrongly insist. It's the root of many living, thriving, ever-changing languages, our own dear English among them. Would you say that the roots of a flowering tree were dead, simply because they were a bit buried? Of course not!"

Nev had been settled in an armchair, its worn cushions perfectly shaped to the curve of the backs of countless students, with Danny next to them. The loose semicircle of chairs was filled with students, all scribbling furiously in their notebooks. Professor Bellairs had a habit of speaking quickly.

"Learning language roots is, of course, of the utmost importance to what we want to achieve with this class," Bellairs continued. "Once you understand a language's patterns, the rhythms that run through them, you'll be able to easily grasp them, master them, and adapt them to your own purposes. In fact, once you've got the underlying roots grown out a bit, you can even create complex language systems of your own."

With an effort, Professor Bellairs hauled himself up from his armchair, smoothing out the rough tweed of his suit jacket as he turned to the chalkboard.

"William Shakespeare himself is obviously a prime example of someone who was able to make great use of language's flexibility. Words and phrases that Shakespeare created for his plays and poems are now in common use today. You've probably heard a lot of them without even realizing it."

He reached up to an empty space on the chalkboard to scrawl the words *What's past is prologue.*

"But one needn't stop at simply adapting a language, when you can use its root patterns to create something more unique."

He scrawled several other lines under the first. The size of each line marked it clearly as the same phrase written above, but the symbols he wrote became increasingly unfamiliar.

All except one line, where Nev recognized a strange, looping script. They stared at it for a long moment, their mind reeling. They slid the small, black leather notebook they'd found in the under-basement out of their pocket to compare to the letters on the board.

They were the same language; Nev was sure of it.

Danny caught Nev's eye, raising a questioning eyebrow at the notebook. Nev shook their head silently at him. *Later.*

The lecture continued and eventually concluded. As the students began the noisy process of shuffling out, Danny leaned over to Nev, his voice low.

"What's going on? You've got this intense look on your face."

"I'm not sure yet," Nev said. "It might be nothing.

I need to talk to Professor Bellairs. I'll catch up with you and tell you if I learn anything."

Danny shrugged, gathered up his papers, and shuffled out with the rest of the students.

With the room mostly clear, Nev approached Professor Bellairs. They tried to muster a casual, friendly air, something they weren't at all used to doing. They attempted this by picturing Danny, and simply doing what they thought he might do.

"Hey, Professor," they said, and immediately flinched at their bold tone, regretting this whole course of action.

Professor Bellairs, who'd been riffling through a stack of books, looked at Nev with a surprised expression on his face.

"Yes, hello," he said. "Remind me of your name?"

"Tallow, sir. Guinevere Tallow," Nev said. They dug their hands deep into their comforting coat pockets. Their class notes were tucked under their arm, but the smaller, mysterious notebook was nestled in their inner upper-left pocket, out of sight.

"Ah, your parents had a taste for the classics and a flair for the dramatic, I see," Bellairs said. "A complicated namesake, that one. From the Welsh, *Gwenhwyfar.* 'The Pale Spirit,' approximately. Represented as either the pinnacle of virtue, however flawed, or a duplicitous traitor. Depending on who's penning the myth, you understand."

"Erm, yes, sir," Nev said, squirming. They weren't really sure how they were expected to respond to this.

Bellairs smiled ruefully, seemingly embarrassed at the tangent.

"I'm sorry. Can I help you with something, Guinevere?"

"Yes, sir," Nev said. They pointed up to the fresh row of words on the chalkboard. "I was very interested in what you had to say about creating languages. I was hoping you could tell me more about this one."

They tapped their finger against the familiar, unreadable writing.

"Ah, so that flair for the dramatic runs in the family, I see!"

Bellairs crossed behind Nev to one of the nearby shelves, running his finger along the spines of the books.

"That particular language is Enochian. It was developed by occultists in the sixteenth century."

He pulled down a slim volume with a hard canvas cover, *The Language of Heaven* stamped in ornate silver across the front.

"It was purported to be the language of angels, or

by some accounts the language of demons, communicated to the original writers via an honest-to-goodness crystal ball."

He turned back to Nev, a mischievous smile on his round face.

"Now, it's not my place to judge anyone's beliefs, but if Enochian is *truly* the language of beings from beyond, then the language construction is curiously similar to English. You'd think the supernatural would have a bit more imagination."

He passed the volume to Nev.

"Luckily for you, this is a fairly new edition. There's been a renewed interest in occult languages of late, what with the ghost-talkers and table-tappers you hear all over the radio these days. What's your interest, if I might ask?"

Nev took the offered book, running their fingers along the cover's sturdy canvas. They thought, briefly, about showing the notebook to Professor Bellairs. Looking up to the professor, to the too-eager gleam that had suddenly appeared in his eyes, Nev thought better of it. For all they knew, Bellairs could know about what was hidden in the east wing. Nev thought it was best to keep the notebook a secret for now, until they knew exactly who it belonged to and what it said.

"Nothing particular," they said. "I just thought it looked interesting."

Professor Bellairs nodded, that eager gleam still dancing in the corners of his eyes.

"It is that. Borrow that, let me know what you think. In fact, why don't you see what you can make of the language? Write a little something in it, bring it to me next time. It will make for a stimulating extracurricular project."

Nev nodded, flipping through the book with interest. There were sections detailing the history of language, theories about the origins of the symbols themselves, and a key for translating the letters and words.

Nev felt a small smile grow across their face. Finally, here was something they could figure out, a puzzle that could be solved. If they could translate the journal, it may lead to more answers about the under-basement, the beast, or any of the other secrets that Deephaven held.

Nev headed off to the dining hall with the textbook under their arm, planning to meet with Danny for lunch and share what they'd learned. They were interrupted when they turned a corner and found Patience standing in the middle of the hall, smiling as though she had been waiting for them.

"There you are. I've been looking all over for you."

Patience's wide and welcoming grin froze Nev to the spot.

"I'm so glad I found you. We haven't had time to talk much since the term began, and I'd *so* like to get to know you better. You haven't been avoiding me, have you?"

Nev felt their guts clench at the thought of disappointing Patience.

"Of course not," they said. "I'm sorry. I've just been busy with schoolwork."

While something about the prefect made Nev want to please her, Nev still had to be careful about who knew about their misadventure in the east wing. She might already know about it from Thaddeus, but Nev couldn't be sure. Patience was in a position of authority, and that meant she was in a position to completely ruin Nev's chance at rebuilding their life.

Patience laughed, an amused fluttering sound.

"Of course you'd be the monastic type," she said. "Studying isn't the *only* important thing at Deephaven, though."

As quick as a snake strike, Patience took Nev's hands in hers, squeezing them gently together.

"That's why I wanted to talk to you. Being a part

122

of the academy means being a part of a *community*. You know what they say; the friendships you make at school will last a lifetime. I want to be friends with *you*, Guinevere."

Nev swallowed. As intimidating as they found Patience, they *did* want to be friends with her too. Nev thought about the way they'd seen the other students trail after Patience, pulled into her wake like dazzled fish. Patience seemed to be everything Nev wasn't: confident and imposing, someone who wasn't afraid to take up space in the world. Maybe Nev just wanted a little of whatever magic Patience had.

Nev managed to nod weakly.

"I wanted to invite you to a little get-together tonight. It's a small thing," Patience said. "It'll just be in my rooms, with a few friends of mine. They'll be so excited to get to know you. Say you'll come."

Some instinct in the back of Nev's head screamed a distant warning; this party had suspicious echoes of Thaddeus's *initiation*. But with Patience's imploring look, all they could do was nod again. They were rewarded with another one of Patience's radiant smiles.

"Excellent! Be at my rooms at the top of the dormitory tower just before midnight tonight. The other first-years will also be joining us. Don't worry about being out of bed after hours; we won't be leaving the dormitories, and being a prefect does have a few privileges."

She winked at Nev, and just as quickly as she'd appeared, she vanished back into the maze of the house's hallways. Nev felt breathless in the wake of Patience's torrent of words. They shook their head, trying to put their thoughts back in order, and went to find Danny.

Chapter Nine

Nev stood in the dark at the top of the winding dormitory stair, listening to the low hum of voices that filtered out of Patience's room with the sliver of amber light beneath the closed door. They'd been trying to gather the courage to knock for the last three minutes. Though they had been invited, Nev couldn't shake the feeling that they were intruding where they weren't wanted. They wondered if Danny was already inside, making friends in his easy way. They wondered if they should just go back to their room.

The decision was taken out of their hands when

the door was flung open, the amber glow spilling out to catch Nev like a spotlight. Patience stood framed in the doorway, wrapped in a sapphire dressing gown that was every bit as elegant as her usual pristine outfit. She looked like an enchantress, here to reveal Nev's fate to them.

"We all got tired of waiting for you to knock." Patience laughed. "The floors of this house are far too creaky for you to be lurking out here without anyone noticing."

Nev flushed. Patience turned back into the room, her gown flowing around her, and Nev obediently followed.

The room was twice the size of Nev's, and was in fact a sitting room, with another door along the far wall presumably leading to the bedroom. The suite was crowded with students. Nev recognized them from classes and mealtimes, though they hadn't spoken to most of them. Scattered among the older students were the faces of a few of Nev's fellow first-years. Victoria spared them a single withering glance from the arm of a large chair where she was perched, deep in conversation with a boy sporting shoulder-length red hair. The top of Beckett's curly hair could be seen tucked in a far corner, his head low and chattering quietly with another boy.

A few of the students wore pajamas or dressing gowns at the late hour, though most, like Nev, still wore the clothes they'd worn to classes earlier that day. They huddled in knots, clustered around the furniture and blazing candlesticks scattered throughout the room.

"Make yourself comfortable, Guinevere," Patience said, her hand on Nev's shoulder. "Introduce yourself to a few people. I've just got a few things to finish setting up, and then we can get started."

"All right," Nev said, uncertain. "What is it we're doing?"

Patience held one slim finger to her lips and winked. "You'll have to wait and see."

She swept effortlessly through the crowd and vanished through the bedroom door, leaving Nev to the tide of strangers. They rocked back on their heels, uncertain of what to do. Nev's hands unconsciously drifted to their pockets, grasping at the mechanical rabbit they'd been working on. It was almost finished; it just needed a little fine-tuning to the jump. Nev itched to tuck themselves into a forgotten corner and lose themselves in an activity that would always make more sense to them.

Failing that, Nev resolved to look occupied by heading toward the snacks. An ornate desk had been made to serve as a buffet table, its surface crowded with dishes. Tiny cups huddled at the base of a steaming silver teapot, and a plate of gingersnaps sat next to a pot of what looked like peach jam. Nev set about the laborious process of assembling a plate and hoped that by the time they were done everyone would have forgotten about their existence.

"Is this your first time at one of Patience's *soirées*?"

The airy voice sounded at Nev's shoulder. The boy with the shoulder-length red hair that Victoria had been talking with stood smiling at them. He wore a dark green knit cardigan that handsomely offset his hair.

"Yes, it is," Nev said. They tried to smile warmly, and worried that it looked more like a nervous grimace. "I'm not really used to late-night parties."

"Oh, you'll love it," the boy said. "Patience's get-togethers are *never* boring. She's very, ah, creative."

He stuck out his hand for Nev to shake.

"I'm Allez. I'm the captain of the fencing team."

"I'm Guinevere. Nev, if you like. I know one of your teammates," Nev said, shaking the offered hand.

"Ah yes, our dear clumsy Mr. Harper," Allez said, sighing. "He actually has great instincts as a fencer. I only wish he'd waited until *after* our first match to try somersaulting down the stairs."

129

Nev felt defensive, guilty at letting Danny take the blame.

"Well, the dormitory stairs *are* a bit narrow, especially in the dark," they said pathetically.

Allez snorted. "You should have seen the stairs when the dorms were in the east wing. You practically had to walk up on tiptoes."

Nev's attention sharpened.

"You used to sleep in the east wing?"

"We all did," Allez said, "before, you know, the accident."

Nev wondered if they were thinking of the same accident. They decided that now would be a good time to find out.

"I heard it was haunted," Nev said carefully.

Allez nodded, warming to the prospect of gossip.

"That's what they say. I knew her, you know."

"The ghost?" Nev said.

"Well, she wasn't a ghost at the time," Allez said. "Her name was Naomi. Tragic, what happened."

"What exactly *did* happen?" Nev said. They didn't have to feign the curiosity in their voice.

"Well," Allez began, leaning close in a conspiratorial whisper, "I was actually one of the last people to see her alive. A lot of people here were; the accident happened right after one of Patience's parties.

We'd been up late. I'd just gotten back to my room and was dozing off when Patience hammered on my door. A support beam or something had cracked, and the whole wing was apparently in danger of coming down."

Nev nodded. Apparently.

"There had been a lot of rain that week," Allez continued. "It must have weakened the foundations or something. I don't know. I'm an athlete, not an architect.

"In any case, we were all rushed out of the tower in the middle of the night. I remember standing in my robe in the main hall and hearing this *terrible* sound from the east wing. Like a thousand voices screaming all at once. I still have nightmares about it. Apparently, that's what it sounds like when a centuries-old floor structure gives way. We'd left just in time. It was only later that morning that we learned poor Naomi hadn't made it out."

"That's awful," Nev said. "And the ghost? You've seen it?"

"Well, not me *personally*," Allez said. "But others have. And sometimes, I think I can hear sounds coming from the east wing, late at night. At first, I told myself it was just the house settling, but . . ."

Allez laughed suddenly, startling Nev.

"You look so serious! It's only a ghost story. Oh look, Mr. Harper has finally decided to join us."

Nev turned to see Danny slipping in through the suite door, looking frazzled. His gaze swept the room before locking onto Nev. He began to stride purposefully toward them, his face filled with urgency, trying to maneuver around the tangled knots of students.

"Your attention, everyone!"

Patience's voice rang high and clear above the hum of the gathering, sending a ripple through the small crowd.

"We're ready to begin."

She had managed to clear a sizable circle in the middle of the sitting room, the nearby students clustered around the edges. She had laid a circle of small, mismatched cushions, at the center of which was a single tall candle perched on a black iron candlestick. Lying beneath the candle was a white lily.

"Everyone come sit in the circle. Don't be nervous. Here, Cecilia, come sit next to me. And, Guinevere, sit here with Ruth. Danny will be all right without you for a moment; let's have you make some *new* friends."

There was a noisy shuffle as everyone took their place, and Nev and Danny were pulled from each other in the tide. Nev settled on a small cushion next to Ruth.

132

Nev recognized her as the girl who had been whispering urgently with Patience, in the dark hall that first night of orientation. Ruth gave Nev a shy, tight-lipped smile, avoiding their eyes while fidgeting restlessly. Nev returned the smile, even as they tried to sort out her place in the puzzle of Deephaven.

As the chaotic shuffling around them died, Nev glanced at Danny over the top of the flickering candle, on the opposite side of the circle. He still looked frazzled, but he shrugged as he settled into his own cushion. Nev wondered what he had been about to tell them.

Patience walked slowly around the outer edge of the circle, extinguishing candles as she went.

"Is everyone comfortable? Good. Then let's begin."

She drifted down onto a large velvet pillow, joining the circle between Ruth and a girl wearing old-fashioned clothes covered in layers of lace. Moonlight floating in through the window behind her cast a pale halo around her hair, contrasting the dim red flicker of the lonely candle.

"Deephaven is an old place," Patience intoned. "It's full of history, and memory, and spirits. Tonight, we are going to reach out to the souls of those who have walked here before and see what wisdom they can share with us."

With a flourish, Patience drew a small box from the pocket of her robe, revealing it to be full of gleaming silver pins. A nervous titter went up from the circle at the sight of the sharp glint.

Patience drew a single pin from the box before passing it to the girl in lace next to her.

"Here, Cecilia. Take a single pin and pass the box around," Patience said. "Don't worry. You'll all be perfectly safe, as long as you do *exactly* as I say."

She flashed her dazzling smile, and again the gathered students laughed nervously.

Nev took the box from Allez, who was seated to their right, drawing out a single pin before passing the box to Ruth on their left. The light of the candle flame caught on the edge of the pin and danced there.

"Pass your pin through the flame three times, slowly," Patience said, demonstrating. The others moved to follow her lead, nearly resulting in a lot of accidental stabbing while they clustered around the candle. Nev waited until there was a bit more space before passing their needle through the flame, feeling the metal heat between their fingertips. They glanced up at the other students in the circle. Their faces looked eager and strange in the flickering light, the walls behind them lost to darkness. Nev hadn't gone to a lot of parties before coming to Deephaven, and they wondered if they were all like this.

"Now, listen very carefully," Patience said. "One after another, prick a single finger with the needle and let a drop of blood fall on the petals of the flower. Our blood will call to the spirits beyond the veil, and the flower will be our gift to them."

Patience pushed the tip of the needle to the end of one slim finger, her face still and unflinching. She used her thumb to squeeze out a single drop, letting it splash on the lily in the middle of the circle. Red leeched into the white petal like ink spreading across paper. The stain was vivid, even in the dim light. Patience nodded to the girl next to her.

"A-are we certain this is safe?" came a small voice in the circle. It belonged to a boy with a fair, sad face and long curling hair. "I mean, I have a friend back home who—"

Patience flashed him a kindly smile.

"Come on, Edgar. Of course it isn't. Otherwise, what would be the point in doing it? But if you're afraid . . ."

She let her voice trail off. Though Nev wasn't the focus of Patience's attention, even they could feel the embarrassment at the idea of leaving early, at disappointing her. Edgar shook his head and dutifully pricked his finger, only the smallest wince skittering across his pale face.

The students pricked their fingers one after the other, and now there was no laughter, nervous or otherwise. The gathering had taken on a quiet air, the feeling of a somber ritual being carried out.

Patience produced a large book bound in a deep green canvas and turned quickly through its stiff black pages, revealing it to be a scrapbook. News clippings with unreadable headlines and scraps of books were pasted to the pages.

Nev caught a quick glimpse of small, yellowed pages as Patience flipped past them. Pages filled with a familiar scribbly handwriting in brown ink. Pages that looked like they belonged in the journal Nev had found.

Patience found the page she was looking for and balanced the book in her lap. She swept her gaze up with a magnanimous smile at the students circled around her. The smile faltered as she locked eyes with Nev.

"Guinevere, aren't you joining us?"

Nev jumped, tearing their eyes away from the scrapbook and the familiar pages. The other students in the circle looked at them expectantly, or in Danny's case, apprehensively. Nev felt the weight of their attention, nodding once before quickly pressing the sharp point of the still-warm pin into their fingertip. A bead of red bloomed there, and Nev let it fall to join the rest among the gory scene of the flower's murder.

"Now, everyone join hands," Patience said. "Let us call out to the night and see what answers."

To Nev's right, Allez gently took their hand. To their left, Ruth gripped their hand tight, her palm sweating. Nev glanced at the quiet girl; she seemed ready to flee the room from panic.

"No matter what happens," Patience intoned, "no matter what you see, don't let go of each other's hands. Don't break the circle. Now, focus on the flame and repeat after me."

She took a deep breath, and the candle flame danced brightly in her eyes.

The blood calls.
The flame guides.
The bloom stalls.
The soul confides.

Patience's voice filled the empty vacuum of silence, replacing it with force. With each successive repetition of the chant, more students joined in. Soon the words rumbled through the floor and into Nev's chest and out of their own mouth.

The blood calls.
The flame guides.
The bloom stalls.
The soul confides.

The chant flowed through Nev, their own voice blending with the others, until it was indistinguishable, until there was only a single, many-throated voice. It was terrifying. It was exhilarating.

The blood calls.
The flame guides.
The bloom stalls.
The soul confides.

Nev let their gaze be drawn to the lone candle, as Patience had instructed. The flame was still, so still that Nev might have been looking at a painting of a candle rather than the real thing. Their vision became a tunnel, narrowing in on the dark that rested in the center of the flame. It was an empty space, hollowed by the light and heat that surrounded it. For a moment, Nev thought the empty darkness was shaped in the silhouette of a person.

Nev felt dizzy.

The blood calls.
The flame guides.
The bloom stalls.
The soul confides.

The world outside of the flame spun. Nev was overcome with vertigo and tore their eyes away, trying to settle their gaze on more solid things. Everyone in the circle continued to stare fixedly at the candle, repeating the chant with that singular booming voice.

Everyone except for Patience, who stared, unblinking, at Nev.

The blood calls.
The flame guides.
The bloom stalls.
The soul confides.

The candle flame flickered once, then went out.

The room plunged into an impenetrable dark. The chant fractured, shattering into terrified yelps and startled laughter. The sudden loss of light caused phantom colors to bloom in front of Nev's eyes. They tried to blink them away and realized that more than the candle had been extinguished; moonlight no longer flowed in through the window. Darkness reigned absolute.

The others in the circle fell into a waiting quiet. The world seemed to fall away, and Nev became disoriented. They tried to pull out of the circle, to reconnect with the solid world, but they couldn't. Ruth gripped their hand in a panicked vise. Nev blinked, trying to see anything but the colors that continued to dance across their eyes.

And then they did see something.

There was a place where the phantom colors would not go, an absence even more absolute than the one that engulfed them. It was a shape cut out of blackness, an impenetrable dark resting in an inescapable void. It stood, in what must be the center of the circle, in the silhouette of a man.

The shape seemed to turn its head, lost and searching. It froze, and the space where a head would be tilted, seeming to listen to some unheard sound. Then it slowly turned its void-face to look directly at Nev.

Nev's blood surged through them, pounding loudly in their ears. The shape seemed to drift closer through the dark, reaching for them. Nev tried to pull away, to flee, but they were trapped. Ruth still gripped at them tightly, terrified, their hand slick with sweat. The shape before them reached out with invisible fingers in a gentle caress, promising oblivion. Nev wrenched against the grip that held them, opening their mouth to scream as they struggled.

Their hand slipped free.

The shape vanished, replaced by a sudden flare of light as the candle in the center of the circle was relit. Everyone squinted against the sudden light and nervous chatter bubbled up to fill the silence.

"Did it work?"

"I think I felt something touch my hair!"

"Look, the flower!"

At the base of the candle, the flower lay beneath the dried brown blood, withered and gray, drained of all life.

Patience stood suddenly, sending the green-bound scrapbook thumping to the floor. Her expression filled with rage, framed by the moonlight that was once again streaming in through the window.

"Who," she said softly, dangerously, "broke the circle?"

Nev glanced at Ruth. The girl's head was bent away from her, long dark hair obscuring her face. Her fists shook at her sides.

Allez suddenly laughed.

"It might have been me, to be honest," he said. "My nose started itching right at the start and it was driving me *crazy*."

Patience's stony glare swiveled toward him as he spoke. Then, like clouds vanishing before the sun, the rage was gone, and Patience's usual cheery demeanor reappeared as though it had never been anything else.

She laughed.

"Sure it did, Allez. I suppose I can't blame you for being a little jumpy. Though if you're all scared of the possibility of seeing a little ghost, you're probably at the wrong school."

A ripple of laughter went through the students, and this time there was no edge of nervousness. The circle disintegrated.

The students drifted back to their knots or to the snack table, and Danny caught Nev's eye from across the room. He shrugged, unsure of what had just happened.

Patience blew out the candle in the center of the shattered circle as the other candles in the room were relit. She gathered it up, along with the desiccated flower and her scrapbook. As she straightened to return the items to her bedroom, she left behind a small black leather pouch, fallen from between the pages of the book. Patience didn't seem to notice, sweeping back into her room with a flutter of her magnificent midnight dressing gown. Smoothly, reflexively, Nev snatched up the pouch, doing it in the same motion as standing up, slipping it safely into one of their coat's many pockets.

The party didn't go on much longer. Danny and Nev exchanged a few words but were soon enough caught in the eddies of students drifting back to their own rooms. Nev found a quiet corner amid all of the movement to quickly peer into the contents of Patience's dropped pouch.

It held a strand of long black hair, woven in an ornate braid around a cluster of three long, sharp teeth.

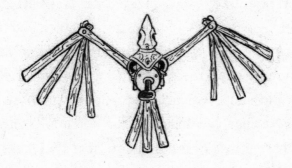

Chapter Ten

Nev leaned away from their small dormitory desk and rubbed their eyes with the heel of their hands, a dull ache pulsing through their skull. Scattered on the desk in front of them were their attempts at translating the small notebook they'd found in the under-basement: scraps of scribbled paper and fragments of sentences. They had the book Professor Bellairs had given them, the pages open to the Enochian translation key.

At the edge of their desk was the small bag Nev had "collected" from Patience's room, its grisly contents presenting another puzzle that Nev wasn't sure they wanted to solve.

For now, they were focused on translating the journal. It was slow and frustrating work, but Nev was determined to mine the little notebook for all its secrets. The more they thought about what little they had glimpsed of Patience's scrapbook, the more sure they were that they had seen the notebook's missing pages pasted inside, and the more sure they were that it could provide at least some of the answers they were looking for.

So far, Nev hadn't learned much. The notebook seemed to be part personal journal, part classroom notebook, part spell book. It had belonged to some long-ago student; the early entries talked about getting used to Deephaven's strange structural mumbling, their difficulty finding friends, the challenge of the classes. As the entries went on, the unknown student had begun to notice things at Deephaven: strange noises in the night, students going missing without explanation, unsettling artifacts of unknown purpose being left in front of their dormitory door, in their book bag, on their bed. The student had begun the journal to record what they were seeing, and to try to unravel the root of it. Nev sensed a kindred, investigative spirit. The fact that the student had decided to write their journal in an occult code was unsettling, but it was clear to Nev that they had done so to keep prying eyes from reading the entries. But who had they thought would try to read it, and why did they go to such lengths to prevent them?

The biggest thing Nev had learned so far was that the dark strangeness at Deephaven had existed for much longer than any of the current students had been there.

They skipped ahead in the journal to the part just before the gap where the missing pages had torn out. They picked their way through the unfamiliar characters, comparing them to the translation key from Professor Bellairs, writing out the results as they went:

> *The possibilities seem endless, but I suspect that is a trap. I will admit that it is a tempting one; to be able to change your shape at will, to mold it to whatever purpose you desire. That is true freedom. But that is why I mistrust it.*
>
> *How easy it would be to lose yourself so completely that you could never find your way back to your own body and mind.*
>
> *I believe I have a solution, though. If I use a ritual to only change into one specific shape, I will be able to better control it. By binding my own*

essence to the essence of whatever form I want to
take, I can use my new shape while preserving the
way back to my old one.
   The key to the ritual is constant contact with—

The rest was cut off by a jagged edge of torn paper. The words, though interesting, held little meaning for Nev without more context. Certainly it told them nothing of immediate use, and they were exhausted. They needed to rest their eyes on something other than strange words in old ink.

They stood up, stretching their stiff limbs, before shuffling their stack of translation attempts and putting them in a drawer in the wardrobe. They picked up the journal, about to slip the familiar weight into their pocket, before deciding that they were sick of looking at the yellowed pages for the day. They put it in the wardrobe as well, locked it, and slipped the key into their pocket. Then they set off to find Danny.

It was beautiful outside, the kind of autumn day that had a chilly breeze but a warm sun. Nev breathed in the fall air, glad to have a moment to step out from Deephaven's occasionally oppressive gloom. The wings of the academy spread out from its stone chapel center, reaching its tall spires and crooked chimneys up into the clear, cold blue sky. The forested hills that sheltered the house on all sides were burnished a blazing gold, the colors of the autumn trees vivid and warm. Nev inhaled again, taking in the late-season smells of damp earth and fallen leaves. The breeze rustled gently through their coat, and for a single contented moment, Nev was able to relax a little.

They found Danny outside as well, along with the rest of the school's fencing team. They, like Nev, had decided to take advantage of the pleasant autumn weather and were practicing on the grounds. Allez was supervising, his long red hair tied back, along with his co-captain, a tall, broad girl whose name Nev thought was Cassidy. The rest of the team stood in a row between them, fencing foils extended. They alternatively lunged forward and danced back to the calls of the team captains, the lengths of the swords glinting silver in the daylight.

Nev settled on a nearby stone bench, its rough surface warmed by the sun. It was easy to spot Danny among the group; he was the tallest in the lineup. He had a new, unbroken fencing foil, sweating even in the cool air as he tried to keep up with the others despite his injury. Nev thought he was doing well, but of course they didn't know the first thing about fencing, so it was hard to tell.

They dug into their pockets for their tools and

drew out a canvas folder of tweezers and screwdrivers and the half-assembled components of their newest project. It would be, when finished, a bird. Nev spread out the components across the empty part of the bench and, with one ear on the fencing practice, got to work.

Screws stolen from broken eyeglasses twisted smoothly into gears from long-dead watches. Bits of discarded wire wound through wheels from broken toys. Slowly, steadily, the form took shape in Nev's hands, building to something whole and complete. Nev felt their mind quiet as the strangeness of the last few days fell away.

This helped. This had always helped. Nev's magpie heart sought and gathered the misplaced, broken parts of the world around them, and their mechanical mind shaped it into something new. In Nev's hands, everything had a use. Everything fit. Everything belonged exactly where it was.

Nev had just set aside the mechanical bones of the would-be bird to lay out the patches of colorful cloth that would become its feathers when Danny plopped down onto the bench next to them, carefully avoiding the mechanical odds and ends. He mopped the sweat from his face with a cloth and beamed happily at Nev in greeting.

"How's practice?" Nev asked.

"It's all right," Danny said, still a little breathless. "It's tough, but I think I'm getting the hang of it. Allez says I'm improving."

Nev glanced up from their work. The fencing team had scattered across the lawn, sipping water or swinging their fencing foils aimlessly. Allez caught Nev's eye from across the field and gave them a friendly wink.

"Is he still mad at you for getting injured?"

Danny shrugged.

"It's not like he can easily replace me. It's a small school, and a smaller team. What are you working on?"

Nev showed him, carefully picking up the mechanical skeleton and inserting one of the many windup keys they collected into its back. They wound the mechanism and set the almost-bird onto the bench between them and Danny. It "flew" smoothly across the stone surface, gliding on wheels hidden beneath its body as its wire and cloth wings flapped. It looped in a few small, graceful circles on the stone bench before it bumped up against Danny's leg. The almost-bird flapped a few more times and went still.

Danny laughed. He picked up the small machine carefully, turning it over to inspect.

"This is incredible," he said. "How did you learn to make this?"

Nev couldn't help but smile at his delight.

"Trial and error," they said. "Mostly error. I started making little toys to, uh, to take my mind off things. My mother and father were fighting a lot then. It felt good, to be able to make something out of the broken things I'd find around the city."

Nev shrugged, trying not to get pulled too far into the past.

"After my mother left, I started making more. It helped, a little. I started selling them, and that helped too, especially when things got bad for my father. I've made a lot of these by now."

They glanced down at the rainbow scraps in their hands that they would soon shape into feathers.

"You can have this one when it's finished, if you want," Nev said on impulse.

Danny glanced up, surprised.

"Really?"

Nev didn't need to sell the toys anymore, not with Deephaven keeping a roof over their head. But they still felt compelled to make them, and the idea of the toys piling up in some corner of their room, just as useless as they had been when they were nothing but bits of discarded junk, made Nev's heart ache.

"Yeah, really," Nev said. "If you'd like. I've still got quite a bit of work to do on it, though."

"Thank you," Danny said. "I'll look forward to seeing it when it's finished."

"I don't see you stretching, Harper!" boomed Cassidy, the team's co-captain, from across the field. She angled a stern brow in Danny's direction. "Do you want to be in fighting shape for our first match or not?"

Danny put the mechanical skeleton back on the bench. He gave his team captain a chagrined smile and carefully stretched the uninjured parts of his arm, wincing a little. Nev drew out a spool of thread to begin stitching the feathers of the would-be bird together.

"The other night, at Patience's party," Nev said, "you looked like you wanted to tell me something."

"Oh!" Danny said. "Right. It's probably nothing. I had an encounter with Thaddeus."

"What did he want?"

"Well, he didn't see *me*, exactly. He was slipping out of the dormitory corridor just as I was heading up to Patience's rooms. I don't think he was invited to the party. He seemed . . . nervous. Like he didn't want to get caught."

"You followed him?" Nev said, a note of incredulity

153

creeping into their voice. They couldn't quite picture tall, beaming Danny engaging in skullduggery on his own.

"He's been acting weird, ever since that night," Danny said. He didn't have to specify which night. "Keeping a low profile, at least around the principal and the professors."

Now that Danny mentioned it, Nev *had* noticed a change in Thaddeus's behavior as well. That first day at Deephaven, Thaddeus had gone out of his way to swan in front of the professors when he wasn't terrorizing the other students. But something had changed after that night. It was as if he suddenly feared the attention, as if he had made some terrible mistake that would cost him if discovered.

"So what happened?"

"He went straight to the east wing door," Danny said. "And that's it. He just stood there, in front of the door. He looked like he was trying to talk himself into going in, or maybe he was listening for something. Anyway, he stood there for a few minutes, clenching and unclenching his fists, before storming off."

"Do you think he's the one who's been sneaking into the east wing?" Nev asked, recalling the window they'd seen wedged open.

Danny shook his head. "He looked scared to me,

like he couldn't stand the thought of going in there. Besides, he doesn't need to sneak; he has the keys, remember? He's hiding *something*, though."

"It seems like everyone in this house is," Nev said. They put aside their sewing and reached into their pocket, drawing out the leather pouch and showing it to Danny. The expression that flashed across his face when they opened it to reveal the coiled hair and teeth could best be described as polite disgust.

"Nev, I know you're in the habit of picking stuff up, but this is, ah, pretty gross."

"It belongs to Patience," Nev said. "It fell out of her scrapbook, which also happens to contain the missing pages from the notebook we found in the under-basement."

Danny's eyebrows shot up. "That's probably not a coincidence."

"No, probably not," Nev agreed. "There are dangerous games being played in this house, and we don't know who all the players are. Someone, probably several someones, is keeping the beast hidden in the east wing. But what does Thaddeus have to do with it, or Patience?"

"What, indeed?" a cold voice purred in their ear.

Nev jumped, drawing the pouch closed and stuffing it quickly into their pocket as they whirled around. Thaddeus stood directly behind them, tall and imposing in a sharp-edged gray suit. He smirked down at them.

"Gossiping, are we? I'd have expected as much from a little thief like you, Tallow, but I'm surprised by *you*, Harper. Giving into the bad influence, I suspect. Now, what were you saying about me and Patience?"

Nev shoved their hands deep in their pockets, trying to keep their expression placid. How much had Thaddeus just heard?

"I was just telling Danny that I've been having trouble finding my way to classes on time," Nev said. "He was suggesting that you or Prefect Patience would be able to help."

"Speak of the devil, and he appears," Thaddeus said with a grin. "As it happens, I've been looking for *you*, Tallow. The principal sent me to fetch you. Come along. I'll help you memorize the route as we go."

He strode off toward the house, confident that Nev would trail after. Nev shared a brief, panicked glance with Danny. They'd been very careful to keep out of the principal's attention, and being called out by her was never good for anyone. Nev scooped up the bits of the mechanical bird and followed after Thaddeus.

The prefect was silent as they walked across the

lobby together, leading Nev deeper into the halls and toward the room where Principal Blanchly gave her weekly seminar. He only spoke when they were far from the usual bustle of the school.

"Now, what were you *really* talking with Harper about?"

Thaddeus didn't turn to Nev, continuing to stride down the narrow hall, the *clack-clack-clack* of his wood heels carrying them forward.

"Sir?" Nev said, in what they hoped was an innocent tone.

Thaddeus whipped around suddenly and shoved Nev, hard. They stumbled, cracking their head against the solid wood wall. In an instant, Thaddeus's hand slammed into the wall beside their head, pinning Nev in place.

"Don't play dumb, Tallow," he hissed. His usual handsome sneer was replaced with a snarling, desperate fury. "I know you saw something in there. What was it?"

Nev blinked, trying to clear their vision of the starbursts that had crowded it when they struck their head.

"Saw something?"

"In the east wing!" Thaddeus spat. "I heard you, just now. Patience is hiding something in there, isn't she? I knew it. What is she hiding, Tallow?"

Nev stared at Thaddeus, and this time they didn't have to feign confusion.

"I know she's already got to you," Thaddeus continued. "She has a type. She likes to gather in all the little lost kids. She likes to make them *dance*."

As he spoke, he tapped one finger again and again near Nev's head in an insistent rhythm.

"I bet she's said all sorts of nice things to you. You've been to her little parties. I used to be invited to those parties too, you know."

"Prefect Thaddeus, I—"

"I know, I know," Thaddeus said. The snarl faded from his face, and his eyes gained a conspiratorial glint. "I don't blame you. She's good at winding people around her finger. An expert. But you won't get anything from *her*. She's nobody. Sure, she's the daughter of some lord or other, but I heard he cut her off. It was a big fight. She's disowned. She has no connections, no influence, no *potential*."

Nev looked at Thaddeus steadily, trying to piece together what he was getting at. It was hard to think with his finger's insistent *tap-tap-tap* next to their ear.

"But me, on the other hand," he said, smiling. "I'm a friend worth having, and a Cuttingham always helps his friends in turn. I could be *your* friend, Tallow."

Nev didn't answer. Thaddeus didn't expect them to.

"Don't say anything now," he said. "I know, I can come off as a little . . . intense. But I think we can be a *big help* to each other. Someone like you, you'll need the kinds of connections I can give you, once we're done with school. I just want to know what dark little secret Patience is hiding in the east wing."

He stepped back, holding both hands out in a gesture of peace as he released Nev. He stood for a moment, expectantly. When Nev didn't say anything, he sniffed impatiently.

"Well, when you feel a little more forthcoming, you come find me. But don't wait too long, Tallow. I won't wait to be your friend forever."

He guided Nev around the corner and down the hall without another word, gesturing them into the lecture hall. As Nev stepped past him, the back of their skull throbbed a dull pain where it had struck the wall.

The lecture hall was much larger than any of the other classrooms in the house. While the others looked like ordinary sitting rooms that had been repurposed for the academy's uses, the lecture hall was built like an amphitheater. Rows of wood benches led down stair-like to the small circular floor below, where Principal Blanchly now stood.

She was tidying the podium she always stood

behind during lectures, straightening papers into concrete rows. She glanced up at Nev as they walked in, her pale gray eyes as blank as a slate.

"Tallow. Come here, please."

"You wanted to talk with me?" Nev said. They tried not to sound apprehensive, even though they were sure that the principal could sense it.

"Yes, indeed," Blanchly said. "How have you been settling in at Deephaven?"

"Um, well enough," Nev said. They weren't certain what the principal wanted to hear, what she already might know. Every interaction with her felt like a test.

"I trust classes aren't too difficult? You're getting along well with the other students?"

"Yes, Principal Blanchly," Nev said. "The academy can be, ah, a challenge. But I'm surviving."

Blanchly gazed at them steadily.

"Let's see that you keep it that way," Blanchly said. "I've heard that you've been making yourself quite at home here. Familiarizing yourself with the house, even the parts that are expressly off-limits."

Nev felt a sickly chill bloom in the pit of their stomach and spread.

"Principal—"

Blanchly held up her hand. "I do not tolerate

excuses. The students at Deephaven are given a remarkable amount of free rein. You are allowed to explore, to direct your attention as you will, and all that is asked of you in return is that you perform to the utmost of your potential, and that you follow our *very* few rules."

The principal crossed in front of the podium to tower in front of Nev, her hands folded menacingly behind her back.

"Deephaven is an old house. It has been a good home to countless students, but like any home, it has its fair share of bad memories. If a place has been made inaccessible to you, it is for a reason."

Nev expected to feel embarrassed, or even frightened. This was the end of their new beginning already. Their future suddenly yawned before their feet, dark and uncertain and terrible. But in the face of that uncertain terror, Nev was faintly surprised to find that what they felt was a reckless defiance.

"I'm just trying to learn new things, Principal Blanchly," they said evenly. "Isn't that why we're here?"

An icy gleam flashed from the principal's spectacles. She leaned down, bending stiffly at the waist until she was eye level with Nev. Her voice was barely more than a hiss.

"You, Tallow, have been extraordinarily *lucky*. But luck does not count for much in this house. You would be wise not to press what little of it you may have left."

She straightened back up soundlessly.

"I am not unsympathetic to your *situation*. But you put yourself willfully in danger. There are parts of the house that simply are not *safe*. I expect you to exercise common sense in the future."

That made Nev blink.

"I'm not expelled?"

Blanchly crossed back to the other side of the podium to resume carving out her stack of papers.

"Not yet," she said. "You have performed adequately in classes. Professor Bellairs has informed me that you've engaged in extracurricular work outside of his lessons. You will be permitted to remain here, for now."

The defiance drained out of Nev, leaving in its place a weary giddiness.

"But I'm warning you," Blanchly continued, "you have found yourself in my attention, and you'll find that can be an *uncomfortable* place to be. Tread carefully, Tallow."

Nev simply nodded, not trusting themself to speak.

Their mind raced as they wound through the halls away from the lecture room. Who had told Principal

Blanchly about their misadventure in the east wing? Thaddeus, or Victoria, or Danny? Nev shook their head at that last. They didn't want to believe that. And how much did Blanchly know about it, about all of it? What else could she be hiding?

Nev was exhausted and decided to head back to their room. They needed some quiet, and maybe a nap, before the evening's classes. They needed to be alone with their thoughts, so they could take them and reassemble them into something whole and complete and useful.

They knew the moment they opened the door to their bedroom that something was wrong. At first, they couldn't pinpoint exactly what. It all seemed normal. The room was empty. The bed was made, the floor was clear, the sun painted thin shadows across their tidy desk. That was when they noticed the problem. The tidiness of the desk was off, incorrect, *not theirs*.

Someone had been riffling through it and had tried to put everything back without Nev noticing.

Nev glanced at the empty hall behind them before closing the door tightly and inspecting the desk. Everything seemed to be there; the pens and papers and keepsakes that weren't practical to carry in their pockets.

Nev had begun to shuffle things into their proper place, confused, when they noticed out of the corner of their eye that the wardrobe hung slightly open. The wardrobe that they were sure they had locked.

Nev's breath lodged in their chest. They stared at the narrow gap between the wardrobe door, looking for any sign of movement hidden within. Vague shapes clustered at the opening, suggesting hunched shoulders and long, slender arms.

They stood still, waiting. Whatever might be in the wardrobe waited, just as still. Nev blinked, eyes dry from staring, and in a sudden rush they darted forward. They flung open the door, even as their other hand dug into their coat pocket, grasping for anything sharp.

But the wardrobe was empty of anything Nev hadn't put there. It had been disturbed, like their desk, though whoever had done it hadn't bothered to try to disguise their searching here.

It didn't take Nev long to find what had been taken. In truth, they had known what it would be the moment they'd realized someone had been in their room and searched their things.

The little handwritten journal was gone.

Chapter Eleven

Nev pulled a vibrant thread through the eye of their needle and began to stitch the colorful pattern of the mechanical bird's feathers. As they stitched, Nev felt their hands steady and their anxious heartbeat slow.

Their room had been broken into, searched, and stolen from. In a house filled with dangerous secrets, Nev had shored up their sense of control, their need for peace, into this room. Now it had been violated, a cracked egg that would let the weirdness seep in.

Nev stitched faster, trying to drown their thoughts in the repetitive motion.

It was late. The gaslights of the house had long since been turned off. Candles glowed from the edges of Nev's desk, large clusters of them lit to beat back the shadows and whatever might hide within them. Beyond Nev's bedroom door the only sound was the house, whispering in its sleep. Nev couldn't keep their limbs still. They needed to focus. They needed to work. They needed a better lock on their bedroom door.

They needed to pee.

Nev had been steadfastly ignoring it for some time now, reluctant to leave even the illusion of security that their room still held. But some things couldn't be put off forever. Nev briefly debated bringing a candle to light their way but decided against it. As much as they were afraid of what lay in the shadowy corners of Deephaven, they were more afraid of becoming a glowing beacon for them. Better to be as unseen as possible.

Nev slid quietly from their room, letting the bright autumn moon light their way down the hall, down the stairs, and to the dormitory's restroom.

After they'd finished, Nev gazed into the gold-framed mirror over the sink. Their hair still hadn't learned to lie flat, though it was getting better, and the dark circles that were always under Nev's eyes were darker from the recent sleeplessness.

However, Nev was surprised to find that, when they looked at their reflection, the face gazing back at them was healthier than the one they were used to seeing. They'd put on weight. Their skin looked warmed and their face more full. Nev actually looked like someone who had been fed and cared for their whole life.

It was disconcerting, but Nev couldn't help but feel a little spark of pride.

Though the arrest of their father had been the tipping point that sent them to seek their new beginning at Deephaven, things at home had been hard for a long time before. Before Nev's mother had walked out of their life, she hadn't been a very attentive person. She used to stand in front of the sink, gazing out the grimy window as the evening light melted into honey, and sigh wistfully. She would stand there long after the light had faded.

And then she'd vanished. Nev's mother had walked into the smoke of the city and never returned, and soon after, the cracks began to show in their already fragile life.

Nev had been left to fend for themself. They had gotten so used to finding their own way, getting their own food, being their own comfort that they could barely remember a time when their life had been any different. For all its secrets and horrors, at least Deephaven provided three square meals a day.

Nev headed back up the stairs, keeping to the pools of moonlight. They finally felt the tiredness they'd been waiting for, the overwhelming desire to just crawl into bed and curl under their heavy quilt.

They reached the landing, and the moon drifting across the floor ahead was blotted out as a dark shape blinked across the window from outside.

Nev rooted to the floorboards, feet firmly within the shadows. Their eyes widened with a barely bridled panic, drinking in the dim light, looking for the barest movement outside . . .

There. Another blot of huddled blackness, moving a window closer and moving fast. Nev turned their head slowly to the next window in the sequence, dreading to see a flash of tangled, oily hair or gleaming, ragged teeth.

Instead, in the passing flurry of movement, Nev glimpsed the hem of a cloak and the toe of a boot. A student. They were outside, headed along some narrow ledge across the window's bottom, sliding carefully away from the direction of the dormitories. In that brief moment, Nev caught a glimpse under the hood of the cloak and saw a serious face almost entirely hidden by a tumble of long dark hair.

It was Ruth, the girl who'd been whispering with Patience in the hall, who'd gripped Nev's hand during the late-night party.

Ruth moved out of sight, not seeing Nev tucked in the shadows inside. The next instant, Nev ran to the nearest window, unlatched it, and swung it open as silently as the old hinges would allow.

Nev had had enough. Secrets lay like stones, threatening to drag down any chance Nev had at making a real life at Deephaven. Tonight, they would start to shed that weight. Tonight, Nev was going to get some answers.

They thrust their head out of the window and into the chill night air. The stone exterior of the house curved out and away from them. The dark figure huddled around the bend and out of sight.

Nev didn't waste time overthinking. Without hesitation, they climbed out of the narrow window and after the figure.

The stony details across the outside of the house provided convenient, if small, handholds and footholds. The stone edge that ran beneath the windows was just wide enough for Nev to slide along, one boot after the other. The occasional gargoyle, leering stonily out at the forest, provided moments to rearrange their grip.

Nev made their steady way forward until Ruth came into sight again, farther along and moving with an assuredness that came with practice. She climbed, deftly and fearlessly, up the far side of the house and into the propped-open third-floor window of the east wing.

At least Nev now knew who was sneaking in. That was one answer.

Clinging to the side of the house's edifice, Nev paused. The east wing reared up before them, a flat darkness crowding at its windows. It was a dark that Nev knew would stink of burned metal and blood, and somewhere within, two pinprick eyes burned brightly.

Nev steeled themself. They'd known, from the moment they saw Ruth dangling outside the dormitory window, where she was headed, and they'd known they would follow her. They knew the secret of the beast would not stay locked behind the east wing door forever, that sooner or later it would pour out and poison Nev's new world. Ruth was tangled up in that secret; Nev was now sure of that, and they needed to know how. As they watched the hem of Ruth's cloak vanish within the open window, leaving the space open, Nev pulled themself forward.

Finally, breathlessly, they made it. Nev clambered

in through the window and dropped onto the floor beyond, their fall cushioned by layers of dust and leaves that had blown in through the open window. Nev lay there for a long moment, breathing, listening intently. They heard the faintest sound, what they thought might be Ruth's careful footsteps, but it was hard to be sure over the rush in Nev's ears.

Eventually, their breathing slowed and their eyes adjusted to the gloom of the east wing. They were in a bedroom, not so different from their own. There was an empty metal bed frame pushed up against a wall, and a squat wardrobe propped up in the corner. Even in the dim light, Nev could see a trail through the dust marking where Ruth had crossed back and forth, heading from the window and out of the door.

Nev stood carefully, straightening their jacket. What was Ruth doing in here?

Now Nev was sure that they could hear her. A gentle rustling came from farther down the hall, as if a large cloth was being unfurled. Nev crept, slow and silent, down the hallway. The whole way, they stared into the shadows, expecting each one to contain a tangled mass that stared back.

All they saw was old wood and dust.

A short flight of stairs led down to a small landing, where the rustling continued. Nev took the stairs walking as close to the wall as possible, so as to avoid creaking. They peered around the side of the banister and saw Ruth.

She knelt, pooled in moonlight, in the center of the curving hallway. A woven blanket was set out in front of her, and Ruth was busy pulling objects from the small bag she carried, placing them around the blanket.

It was all food. Small loaves of bread and slices of meat pie wrapped in a napkin, ham and boiled eggs. Ruth spread it all before her, as if she were laying out a picnic for herself and a friend.

Having finished assembling her spread, Ruth crouched, hands in her lap, and began to hum. It was a soft sound, barely even tuneful. The sound spread itself through the waiting silence of the east wing.

Out of the silence crawled the beast.

Its long, clawed fingers reached into the moon-light at the far end of the hall, its hairy shape pulled from the surrounding darkness. It came toward Ruth slowly, its oily hair dragging faint trails through the dust. Its movements were smooth and careful, a pred-ator who didn't want to spook the prey too early.

Tak-a-tak-a-tak . . .

Then the smell reached Nev, the iron stench burn-ing their eyes. They blinked back tears, staring at the unfolding disaster before them. Ruth didn't move, facing down the hall away from Nev and toward the beast. She didn't stop humming.

The beast stalked closer, and now Nev could see the pale gleam of its teeth, already set in a snarl.

"It's all right," Ruth said softly. The change in sound made the beast flinch, and a noise choked out of its chest, something between a growl and a sob.

"It's all right," Ruth said again. "It's only me. You remember me, right? I know you do. Come here. I've brought food, see?"

Her chatter was continuous, soft and steady. She reminded Nev of a tamer trying to soothe a startled animal.

"You're hungry, right? You must be. Come on. Come and see what I've brought you."

The beast shuffled forward again, stretching out its elongated maw to snuffle at the food spread before it. In a sudden flurry of movement, its jaws opened and meat vanished between its teeth. It began to tear into the midnight picnic with a ferocious hunger.

As it ate, Ruth carefully picked up one of the slices of meat pie and stood, very slowly. The beast's gleaming eyes followed her in the dark.

"Are you ready this time? Come with me. Come on. There will be more food. Please, just follow me. I won't let anything bad happen to you."

She took a step backward, in Nev's direction. Nev pulled back into the shadow of the stairway. They had been preparing themselves for the beast to attack Ruth, though what they would have done, they didn't know. But they had not expected this.

Ruth backed up another step, luring the beast back the way she'd come, toward the way out of the house.

Nev's eyes were wide with confusion even as dread coiled in their stomach. What was Ruth trying to do?

Ruth took another step, and the beast followed, hair dragging along the ground and teeth bared in a warning snarl.

"Come with me. It will be all right, I promise. Please come with me this time. You can't stay here. You can at least be free."

Ruth's voice choked with sudden emotion, a hitch in her calm, even tone.

"I miss you. Oh, Naomi, I miss you so much."

The beast froze, and so did Nev. The entire house seemed to hold in a breath.

Pieces of information began to slide into place in Nev's mind. The missing girl, the lies about why the east wing was locked, the strange things they'd seen in the under-basement and in Patience's rooms.

A terrible, nauseous chill spread through Nev's limbs. They felt sick.

"Please, *please* come. I'll take you out of here. Naomi, please."

The beast cocked its head. That sound came again, the almost-sob. It stepped forward.

Tak-a-tak-a-tak . . .

There was something awkward about its movement, an unsteady sway. Ruth noticed the same instant that Nev did, and air hissed through her teeth.

"You're hurt," she said.

Panic and anger flared at the edge of her voice, and the beast reacted to it. It crouched low, baring its curving fangs. Nev could see it now, a dark gash running under the beast's tangle of hair where Danny had slashed at it.

Ruth cursed herself and immediately smoothed her tone, forcing it back into a placid calm.

"It's okay. I'm sorry. I'm sorry they hurt you. Just come with me, I'll keep you safe. I'll never let anyone hurt you again."

It was too late. The beast coiled in on itself for an instant before it exploded toward Ruth. Ruth emitted a strangled yell and just managed to duck below the beast's outstretched claws, scrambling to its other side.

"Naomi, please, it's all right. It's just me. Please, Naomi, *please* remember me."

The beast whirled around, eyes burning, and loomed over Ruth. Nev stepped out from the stairway, heedless of the noise they might make, their mind racing as they moved to stop what was about to happen.

Ruth choked out a sob as she reached into her pocket.

"I'm sorry, Naomi."

From her pocket she pulled a small bell, the kind with a clapper. It was the same kind of bell that was strung across the east wing door.

Ruth rang the bell, high and clear. The beast flinched back immediately, a scream ripped from its throat as if the ringing was causing it physical pain. It crouched low, throwing its long fingers around its head. Ruth stood, still ringing the bell, tears appearing at the corners of her eyes. The beast turned, unable to bear the sound, and clattered away from her down the hall.

Straight into Nev.

Nev was knocked flat by the impact, their head hitting the floorboards hard. They opened their mouth to cry out in pain and were immediately gagged by the overpowering stench of blood and metal. The beast's

177

oily hair tangled around Nev's limbs. Above them, its gleaming eyes opened wide, the burning blue ringed with white. The expression in its eyes looked angry and hurt and scared. The eyes looked almost human.

The beast screamed, and Nev screamed with it.

Every cell in Nev's body cried out for them to flee, to do whatever was necessary to get away from this thing that had once been a girl. They punched up on instinct. Their fist collided with ragged hair and leathery skin stretched tight across bones. The beast ignored it, its long fingers scrambling at Nev's face and arms, its black claws leaving thin red trails across their skin.

Nev punched again, and this time they felt something wet as their fist connected with the wound Danny had left. The beast screamed again, the sound pained and horribly human. It scrambled away from Nev, leaving Nev's knuckles covered with its dark blood.

Nev didn't waste a moment. Their fingernails dug into the wood floorboards as they pulled away. Across the writhing, matted shape of the beast, Ruth stood staring at them, eyes wide, the bell hanging limp and silent in her hand.

Nev ran.

It felt like a reoccurring nightmare. Nev ran as

fast as their legs would carry them, but it felt like they moved so terribly slow. It was all the same as before: the darkness, the curving hallways, the stench, the sound.

TAK-A-TAK-A-TAK!

Nev's panicked thoughts dissolved into static. All they could do was run; all they could think was *get away*. The walls of the east wing flashed by them, fragmented and meaningless, and soon they were at the open window. Nev climbed out, acting as much by instinct as by sight or touch. They clung to the stony edifice, trying to move as far and as fast as they could away from the horror clutching at their heels.

Long, hairy fingers and ragged black claws reached through the window, scrambling at the sleeve of Nev's coat. Nev yanked away and their grip on the stones of the house slipped.

They fell.

Nev slammed into the sloping tile of the small roof below, the hard slate knocking the breath from their lungs. They rolled helplessly along the slope, sliding again out into empty air. They struck the ground, and at last the smell of iron and blood was replaced with dirt and grass. Everything hurt.

The world went black.

Chapter Twelve

Boom, boom, boom!

Fists pounded on the thin wood of the apartment door, rattling it in its frame. Nev stood in the dim hallway, framed by the ray of honeyed light leaking in through the kitchen window. They gripped a tiny mechanical mouse in their hands, nearly finished. The mice were the most popular, the best sellers of the toys Nev cobbled together and sold on the patchwork quilt they spread out in the park. They still needed to put the finishing touches on this mouse and make a few more besides. Rent was due.

Boom, boom, boom!

"Theodore Tallow!" a voice boomed from outside. "We

know you're in there. Your payments are six months late. Open up, Tallow, this instant!"

It was happening again. Behind Nev, they heard their father stir. It was late afternoon, but he'd been sound asleep. He hadn't been sleeping well at night, not for a long time.

The pounding at the door continued, and hulking shapes crowded in against the door's frosted glass pane. Despite Nev's best efforts, it was all happening again.

"Guinevere?"

Their father's drowsy voice floated down the hall, a useless counterweight to the din at the front door.

"Sweetheart, tell whoever that is to come back later, won't you? My head hurts."

"Mr. Tallow," a new voice said from the other side of the door. It was different from the first voice, quieter, filled with an iron authority. "Open the door now, or we will be forced to break it down."

Nev wanted to scream, or cry, or simply dissolve into the last of the golden afternoon light. They didn't know what scheme their father had tangled himself up in this time, what "sure thing" he'd wasted their money on and brought these angry men to their door. It didn't really matter. Nev would have to take what little money they'd managed to hide away, stitched into the pockets of their coat, and use it to bail out their father. It had happened before, and now it was happening again. In that moment,

Nev drowned in the certainty that it would keep on happening forever.

The door smashed open, sending a small crack across the surface of the frosted glass pane. Three men stood in the hallway outside: a red-faced man with a drooping mustache, in a tan suit that didn't fit him right, and two men in dark uniforms, their faces set with a practiced, neutral disinterest. One of the uniformed men turned his gray shark eyes on Nev.

"Is your father here?"

The men didn't wait for Nev to respond. They pushed past, heading into the dimness of the tiny apartment. Nev stepped out of the light and pressed their back against the cool wall. They shoved their hands deep in their pockets, grasping at the comforting weight of the tools and components that nestled there. Their hand crumpled a piece of paper, an envelope. It had arrived in the mail a few days earlier, addressed to Guinevere Tallow. They hadn't been sure what to make of it, sure it had to be a mistake or a joke. They'd barely even thought of it since then. But they'd kept it, secreted it away with the rest of their things.

The men reappeared at the end of the hallway, their arms locked on either side of Nev's father. He was still wearing the clothes he'd been wearing the day before, rumpled from having been slept in. He blinked irritably at the people crowding his hallway.

"All right, all right," he grumbled. "I can walk on my own, thank you very much."

"Time's up, Tallow," said the mustached man from the doorway. "I've been more than patient. Either pay me what you owe me or you can settle your debt with these fine gentlemen here."

Theodore Tallow sighed.

"There's no need to be so dramatic," he said. "You'll get what you're owed, I just need you to be patient a little—"

"I've been patient," the man with the mustache said. "I'm done. And so are you."

He stood aside to let the uniformed men march Theodore Tallow out of the small apartment. Nev's father looked annoyed, as though this were simply one of the irritations one must bear once in a while. He turned to Nev as he was pulled past them. Nev already knew what he was going to say.

"Sorry about all of these theatrics, sweetheart," he said. "Um, I imagine you have a bit saved up, right? Why don't you come by the courthouse a little later. I know it's tedious. Just meet me there with the money, and we can put all this unpleasantness behind us."

Nev knew just how much they had saved. They had told themself, as they always did, that they were saving it to improve things, to make life at home better. But really, it was just enough to keep the landlord happy if rent didn't materialize, or to pay the bail if their father's debts came knocking.

Or to get a train ticket.

"Guinevere?" their father said when they didn't answer. He smiled at them from between the concrete shoulders of the uniformed men. His eyes crinkled at the edges in the way they always did, filled with a familiar apology and a familiar promise. "You'll meet me there, won't you?"

This had all happened before.

The letter felt heavy in Nev's pocket.

"No," they said. "Not this time."

For a moment, Theodore Tallow continued to smile, a father indulging his child's bad joke. The smile slowly melted in the face of Nev's stony expression.

"Guinevere?"

"Come on," one of the men said, his tone flat. He and the other man pulled Theodore Tallow away, and only then did he begin to struggle. He craned his neck back, searching the face of his child, fear finally bleeding into his eyes.

"Guinevere? Guinevere, please!"

Then he was gone. One of the uniformed men pulled him down the hall and out of sight, followed closely by the smirking man with the mustache. The other lingered in the doorway.

"Someone will be by to collect you a little later," he said.

"You'll be fine until then. I'd pack a bag in the meantime if I were you."

"That's all right, there's no need," Nev said, their voice as flat as the man's. Somewhere in the back of their head, their father's terrified, betrayed voice rang out again, but Nev smothered it into silence. They reached into the pocket of their coat and drew out the heavy, official-looking letter, holding it up for the man to see.

"I'm headed to boarding school today."

Emblazoned across the top of the page was a crest showing an overgrown wand lain across an open book. Beneath it, in neat script, was written:

Dear Guinevere Tallow,
    We are pleased to be writing you with an invitation to continue your education with us at Deephaven Academy . . .

It was a long time before Nev was able to open their eyes. It felt like they were coming from a long way away, trying to surface from the terrible nightmare that was also a memory.

Eventually the wash of pale blue autumn sky filled their vision. Nev held up their hand against the morning light, and their skin matched the cold hue of the sky behind it.

Nev sat up stiffly. What they could feel of their limbs was chilled and damp. They had been curled under the dubious shelter of their big green coat, atop a pile of damp leaves. The woods stood silent on all sides, spreading out into the distance to be reduced to watercolor splotches in the morning mist. Deephaven was nowhere in sight.

Nev didn't remember lying down to sleep. What little they did remember of the night before was just fragments, distorted by pain and darkness and fear.

They remembered a haze of pain as they lay on the grass in front of the house after falling, forcing the cold night air into their lungs one breath after another. They'd stared up at the cutout shape of the academy, its towers silhouetted by the starry sky above them. A black, ragged shape watched them from the narrow window far above, its eyes points of pale blue that matched the stars overhead.

The thought of returning to the house that held such a terrible thing, not just a monster but something worse, had wiped Nev's mind blank with sheer animal panic. They'd stood, ignoring their body's pained protest, and limped away from Deephaven's looming shape. They didn't know where they were going; they only knew they had to get *away*.

They had stumbled into the woods, thinking they could find help, or the road to town, but not really thinking at all, just leaving. Again.

The house had muttered uneasily to itself but remained still. It was content to wait, as it always was.

Now, Nev stood up from the damp, leaf-strewn earth, wincing at the motion. Their body felt like one giant bruise. They pulled their coat on tightly and looked around at the mist-shrouded woods.

With the horror of the previous night blunted by the cool, quiet morning, Nev's mechanical mind began to work properly again, and they considered their next steps. Perhaps they would find the road and follow it to the town, try to find somewhere else, start from scratch again. Maybe the road wouldn't end and they'd simply walk forever. Perhaps the woods would keep them, and someday someone would find Nev's bones huddled beneath what remained of their beloved coat.

Nev started moving, walking through the uneven forest ground, motivated more by a need to warm their frozen limbs than by any solid plan.

In the heart of the woods was a house. Locked

within the house was a beast. Locked within the beast was a girl, as lost and as frightened as Nev was. They'd seen it in its—her—eyes. Those pale, gleaming eyes had burned into Nev's mind. Nev saw them whenever they shut their own eyes now, even to blink. They had recognized the expression in those eyes. They knew what it was like to be trapped.

It had been easy for Nev to leave home, in the end. All they had to do was nothing as their father was dragged away. All they had to do was stand by as the last shabby fragments of their old life fell apart. Their mother was gone, their father was gone, and Nev had let it happen. They had nothing left, but at least they were no longer trapped.

Now, it had happened again. The walls had closed in and Nev had slipped away, alone, leaving the ruins behind.

Nev wondered, not for the first time, if they were a bad person.

They walked aimlessly through the forest, tucking their cold hands into their coat pockets. Nev's fingers bumped against a familiar metal object: the nearly finished toy that nestled inside. They drew it out, gazing at the skeleton of the mechanical bird, miraculously undamaged in their fall from the night before. Its scrap-cloth feathers sat on the desk back in their room, waiting to breathe the final life into the thing. Danny would have liked it, Nev thought.

Danny.

Danny, with his cheery smile and trusting nature. Danny and his chatter and his sword and his just-as-broken childhood. Danny, who had only wanted to be their friend.

Nev stopped walking, gazing down at the toy. When Nev had fled into the woods, they'd abandoned Danny to the mercy of Deephaven's secrets. *He* was alone now, with no clue as to where Nev had gone or what had happened to them.

Things had changed since Nev had left home. This time could be different. They didn't have to choose between being trapped and being alone.

Nev looked around, trying at last to get their bearings in the woods, and spotted a steep slope nearby. Nev climbed to the top of the hill, which was mostly bare save for a few scattered trees. They were able to easily spot what they were looking for; in the distance, far but not nearly as far as Nev would have thought, a single column of white smoke, rising from Deephaven's kitchens as breakfast got underway.

Nev wouldn't run away, not this time. They wouldn't abandon Danny, or the girl trapped within the beast. Nev had abandoned and been abandoned enough. For once, they were going to really fix something. They were going to beat back the shadows held within the house.

They were going to give Danny the toy they'd promised to him.

Nev fixed the location of the column of smoke in their mind. They set off down the hill, through the woods, and back toward Deephaven Academy.

❦

Nev was able to slip back into the academy without too much notice. Breakfast had finished and students crowded the hallways on their way to their first classes of the day, allowing Nev to join their tide. The others paid little attention to them beyond the odd glance at the leaves still stuck to their dew-damp hair.

Nev found Danny waiting for them in their room. He was pacing across the small floor, bouncing on his heels in agitation. Nev stepped into the room, and the sight of their friend lit a smile on their tired face.

"Hi, Danny," they said.

Danny whirled around, his eyes wide in surprise and delight. "Nev!" he cried.

He reached Nev in one long stride, nearly lifting them off of their feet in an awkward one-armed hug, as he tried with little success to keep his sling-wrapped arm out of the way.

"You're all right," Danny said, his voice coming from over Nev's head and rumbling through his chest in the embrace. "I got so worried when I didn't see you at breakfast, I looked all over. I hadn't seen you since Thaddeus took you to see the principal. I thought she expelled you! I thought—"

He pulled away, and Nev was surprised to see he had tears in his eyes.

"I thought you left."

Nev nodded. "I'm sorry," they said. "I did leave. But I'm back now."

"What happened?"

"I had a *really* bad night," Nev said with an exhausted sigh. "Come on, I'll tell you all about it over lunch. I'm starving."

The dining room was mostly abandoned at that hour, with most of the other students in class. Apart from Nev and Danny, there were only a couple of students in aprons scurrying about in preparation for lunch, under the stern, unwavering gaze of Lin, the house's chef. Nev realized that they'd never actually seen Lin before, as she rarely came out of the kitchens. She was a squat woman with impressive arms and a hawk's stare, and an apron with pockets that seemed

192

to be filled with various jars of dried herbs. The chef turned her attention on them as they entered the room, sweeping them up in an appraising glance. She made a disapproving noise at Nev's haggard, hungry appearance and gave a single gruff nod to the beginnings of lunch spread on the table, before turning and vanishing back into her culinary den.

Nev and Danny sat at their usual spot, the warm light spilling in and pooling around their table, burning away the darkness of the previous night. Nev sipped at a steaming cup of flowery black tea, having just piled a plate full of everything that had been on offer.

They told Danny what they'd seen in the east wing. It felt surreal to describe such terrible things between bites of the kitchen's excellent club sandwich.

Danny stared at them, his face frozen in a horrified expression.

"The beast *is* the missing girl? You're sure?"

Nev nodded.

"I didn't believe it when Ruth said her name. I thought Ruth was, I don't know, grieving her friend. There was so much pain in her voice, and I thought it was making her see things. But then the beast found me, and I looked into its eyes and—"

Nev shuddered despite the warm sun, remembering that frightened blue gleam.

"It—she is dangerous. She's like a scared animal. But she's human, or at least some part of her is. I think Naomi is still in there somewhere."

Danny sat back in his chair, letting out a long sigh.

"This . . . this is too much. How does something like this happen?"

Nev sipped slowly at their tea, turning over in their mind what they'd seen and heard. They'd been putting the pieces together since their walk back through the woods, assembling the fragments of information into something more complete.

The missing pages of a mysterious journal, the pages pasted into Patience's scrapbook. The bell-strung door to the forbidden east wing, the small bell in Ruth's hand as she stood within that same tower. The missing girl. Patience's late-night parties. It almost fit together, parts of a set, a puzzle that Nev could bring together to see the full picture.

Nev took another steadying sip of their tea before leaning forward, lowering their voice to ensure that no one would overhear.

"Think of what we found in the under-basement," they whispered. "Think of what happened at Patience's party. Deephaven is a strange place, Danny, and now I think it might be even stranger than we thought."

"Magic," Danny whispered back, shaking his head.

Nev nodded. It felt weird to even be seriously talking about it, but there it was.

Danny slumped back in his seat.

"I can't believe this. Magic is real, and it's terrifying."

Nev could only agree. The two sat in silence, thoughtfully chewing over their food and their new perspective on the world.

"Poor Naomi," Danny said finally. "She's been locked in the house all this time. Everyone thinks she's dead."

"Ruth knew," Nev said. "Ruth has known this whole time. She must have some idea what turned Naomi into *that*. We need to talk to her."

"I haven't seen her today," Danny said, "but I wasn't looking. She kind of keeps to herself, you know?"

"We have to find her," Nev said. "We have to talk to her before it's too late. I think she's trying to let the beast—Naomi—out of the east wing."

"Why would she do that?"

"Because Naomi is trapped," Nev said. It was strange, to feel sympathy for a thing that had tried twice to claw them apart. "She's scared. I think Ruth believes it will help if she's at least free, but it won't. It's just going to get people hurt. Maybe Ruth, maybe other students, certainly Naomi. We have to do something."

"Ruth saw you last night," Danny said. "She knows that you know. She won't want to be found, not by you, if she even *left* the east wing last night. Maybe she got eaten."

Nev paused in midsip of their tea. They didn't want to think such a terrible thought.

"If we can't find Ruth, then we should find Patience. She's the one who stole the journal from my room, I'm sure of it. She already had pieces of it; she would want the rest. She's involved in all of this somehow."

"Nev, if that's true, what makes you think she'd tell you?"

Nev drew out the black leather pouch from her coat pocket, its grisly contents secure within.

"She'll want *this* back."

Danny bent forward across the table, leaning on his elbows, the afternoon light framing his dark curls. He looked around the room conspiratorially.

"Are you sure about this? It's looking like she's really involved in all this. She might be some kind of *witch*."

Nev turned the pouch over in their hands. Within, they could feel the ridges of the teeth, feel the texture of the hair that bound them together. Nev wasn't sure where the teeth had come from, but they were pretty sure they knew whose hair it had been.

"You're right," Nev said. "But Patience *lives* here. She's most likely to know what happened, and she might know how to undo it."

Danny chewed on his lower lip for a moment. Then he nodded. "All right. Then let's go see what Patience knows."

He stood up but froze when he saw that Nev wasn't moving. Nev was unable to meet his eye, staring instead at the gritty dregs of their tea sifting softly at the bottom of the cup clutched in their hands.

"Danny," they said. "You don't need—I don't want you to get hurt again. I'm sorry that I left, but I think I can handle this. You don't have to get any more involved. I don't need—"

Nev stuttered to a frustrated stop, unable to find the right words. Danny didn't say anything but simply waited for them to continue.

"I'm not used to needing help," Nev said finally.

Danny moved to stand beside Nev, placing a gentle hand on the back of their chair. Nev finally looked up at him.

"Of course you are," he said, smiling. "We all need help. You're just not used to getting it."

Chapter Thirteen

Nev and Danny went through the rest of the school day as if everything were normal. Nev couldn't afford to be absent without an excuse, since they were already on thin ice with Principal Blanchly. As they cycled through the familiar pattern of classes, Nev kept an eye out for Patience, looking for their opportunity.

Danny was right; it was unlikely that Patience would just tell Nev what they needed to know. But there were other ways to get the information, and Nev's fingers itched to do a little "collecting."

The opportunity came between the final class of

the day and dinner, when students had a few hours to themselves to unwind or catch up on studies. As everyone poured into Deephaven's hallways, chatting noisily, Nev spied Patience's pale hair over the sea of students. The radiant prefect was surrounded by her usual crowd of admirers, smiling and laughing. She seemed to be a natural point of gravity that drew others to orbit around her. She said something that Nev couldn't hear, causing the people around her to laugh uproariously. Even other students farther down the hall chuckled, afraid of being left out of a joke they hadn't actually heard.

Patience excused herself from the circle of bubbling students, smiling politely as she drifted toward the library on her own, a stack of books under her arm. Nev, who was tucked in the shadow of a nearby doorway, got a close look at the books and noted a familiar scrapbook bound in green canvas. Nev caught Danny's eye among the chaos of students, and together they both followed Patience from a distance down the hall.

The purple glow of the early twilight shone velvet through the library's tall colored-glass windows. Several students were scattered in their own quiet study corners. The librarian sat in their usual place behind the front desk, their wire-rimmed glasses reflecting the words of the novel they were buried in.

Nev and Danny slipped in through the library door, immediately ducking behind some nearby shelves, balancing the need to not look suspicious with the desire to not be seen. Patience had begun to spread out her books at a table tucked between two shelves. She turned to start pulling down more references to add to her stack, eventually bringing her out of her chosen alcove and to the surrounding shelves.

"Keep an eye on her. I'll be quick," Nev whispered to Danny. They needed to get a closer look at the scrapbook before it vanished back into Patience's rooms and out of their reach. They hoped they would only need a moment to see if they could discover what exactly had been done to Naomi, and if it could be undone.

As soon as Patience turned out of sight around a nearby shelf, Nev began to stride toward her study table, as quietly and as casually as they could.

Danny grabbed their arm suddenly, pulling them back into the shadowy alcove.

"Wait!" he hissed.

Around the corner came the unmistakable *clack* of Thaddeus's wood-heeled shoes. He strode into view, looking even more superior than usual. Nev and Danny watched from their corner of the library as

Thaddeus craned his head around the shelves to find Patience.

"Well, *there* you are," he said.

Thaddeus's voice was bright and mocking and loud, earning him a withering glare from the librarian.

"Here I am," Patience said flatly.

She came back into Nev's view, carrying a fresh armload of books. She brushed past Thaddeus without a glance, settling herself into an armchair and adding the books to her stack.

Thaddeus stood in front of her, his arms crossed imperiously.

"You've been avoiding me."

Patience flipped open one of the many books spread in front of her.

"I have literally not thought about you once today."

"Of *course* not," Thaddeus said. "You're too busy, aren't you, little Miss Popular? You're Blanchly's favorite *this* year. She's got you running all over the place lately, hasn't she?"

Patience sighed. She settled back in her armchair and crossed her arms to match Thaddeus.

"Can I help you with something, Thaddeus? Or are you just feeling a little fragile today?"

Thaddeus drew himself up.

"I'm feeling fine," he said. "Wonderful, in fact. I'm just concerned about *you*."

"Well, I have good news for you then," Patience said. "I have, up to this point, been having a lovely day. Now that we've cleared that up, you can go."

"I'm concerned," Thaddeus continued, ignoring her, "that all the pressures of being a prefect are getting to you. We both know how demanding it can be, what a high standard we're held to. I wonder, would you still be the principal's favorite if she knew about your little secret in the east wing?"

Patience's attention sharpened on him like a sudden dagger.

"What did you just say?"

Her reaction seemed to please Thaddeus; even with his back to them, Nev could hear the triumphant smile in his voice.

"You think you're the only one with friends around here? Mine tell me things too, and your little secret isn't going to be secret much longer."

Like a snake striking, Patience's arm whipped out, seizing Thaddeus's necktie and forcing a pathetic *gelp* sound from him. She stood and, with the same motion, slammed Thaddeus's back against the bookshelf, hard. She pinned him there, just out of sight of the librarian, who glanced up at the sound of the collision. For an instant, Nev could feel Patience's sudden burst of rage pulse out like a physical wave, shuddering through the space.

Patience glanced out of the alcove where she had Thaddeus pinned, just as Nev and Danny pulled back farther into the shadows.

"You and I are going to have a long-overdue chat," Patience hissed, almost too quiet for Nev to hear.

Without another word, Patience turned on her heel, her hand still in a vise grip around Thaddeus's tie, and marched him toward the spiraling stairs that led to the more secluded upper floor of the library. As they went past, Nev caught a glimpse of Thaddeus's face, which held a mix of indignant rage and panicked regret.

As soon as the two prefects were out of sight, Danny stepped from the shadows.

"I'll keep an eye out for them. Go see what you can find," he said.

He trailed discreetly after Patience and Thaddeus, following them up the stairs.

Nev didn't waste any time and strode over to Patience's table of books. It was now or never.

They glanced at the titles that Patience had pulled from the shelves as they shuffled them out of the way. There were a few old astrological almanacs, a book on botany, and several books in languages that Nev didn't understand. Patience was known to have a talent for languages. Some of the books seemed to be primers on the languages themselves, while others Nev was unable to glean their purpose. Nev ignored them, focusing on the task at hand. It wouldn't be long before Patience came back, and after the burst of rage that Nev had just seen, they didn't want to be caught riffling through her things.

The scrapbook itself was filled with stiff black pages, buckled by glue and ink. The pages were tabbed, the sort that were designed to allow things to be mounted onto them, and the binding was made so that more pages could be added. Small white tags ran along the edge of the pages, dividing them into sections. Even in their haste, Nev admired the organization.

Pasted into the scrapbook was an eclectic collection: yellowed pages from old books, newspaper clippings with torn edges, ink-stained pages of handwritten text. Some of them were written in English, though most were in Latin or French or German, and other languages Nev couldn't read. Some of them bore diagrams of dense mathematical equations, detailed sketches of plant and animal anatomy, or what looked like bizarrely illustrated shopping lists. Pasted alongside some of the clippings were seeds or stones or small clippings of hair. On the black page margins around each clipping and artifact was dense, neat handwriting. It seemed to be Patience's personal annotations, inscribed in brilliant white ink.

Nev flipped through the scrapbook, quickly and carefully, keeping an ear out for sounds from the library floor above.

They soon found what they were looking for: the small journal pages, torn along one edge, covered in that strange, looping script. Nev had been right; they were the perfect match for the journal they'd found. There were only three pages, mounted in a neat row across the open spread of the scrapbook.

Nev bent low over the scrapbook, trying to quickly read through Patience's dense handwriting. There were mentions of a ritual, one of transformation and change. "Sympathetic binding," one column called it. Nev ran their finger along the edge of the page, keeping their place as they read as quickly as they were able.

- *Dev. possible further applications. Possible to transform into multiple shapes?*

- Willing subject required. Subject must necessarily be trusting and trustworthy. Consider options: Cassidy, Thaddeus, Edgar, Naomi, Alexis.

- Sympathetic binding must be compatible with subject/location. Convenience a factor.

Beneath these notes was an ink sketch depicting several fanged teeth. Drawn next to them was a diagram on a very complex-looking braid, directions on a particular kind of knot to be woven around the teeth.

Next to those was a drawing of a hand bell, the kind that Nev had seen Ruth use, with *x3* written next to it.

Nev turned the page. Steps to a ritual had been written, but then crossed out with a disturbing violence. Beneath the spatters of white ink and jagged paper, Patience's usual handwriting continued.

- **UNFORESEEN CONSEQUENCES.** Unbinding unsuccessful. Result permanent? Incompatibility with binding, subject's will wavered, architectural interference? Further dev. needed.

Nev flipped the pages back and forth. There were no signs of other pages from the journal, though on the back side of the last page there were what looked like more notes and formulas, all variations on the components of the failed transformation. Patience had been working at it, trying to change it or reverse it or re-create it, but it seemed all attempts had failed. Lines were crossed out, descriptions of formulas left incomplete.

A series of sharp wooden *clacks* caused Nev to look up, drawing farther back into the shadows of the bookshelves. Thaddeus came into view, his expression murderous and his tie slightly askew. He seemed to have found another student to take his frustration out on, who trailed after him with an armload of books. Nev was so concerned with looking for any sign of Patience that they didn't immediately notice that the poor student was trying to make eye contact with them.

It was Danny, his expression a mix of chagrin and panic as he tried to get Nev's attention.

Nev quickly shut the scrapbook and piled the other books on top of it, trying to remember the order that Patience had stacked them in. As casually as they could, with their heart hammering in their ears, Nev stepped out of the alcove.

They ran directly into Patience.

The prefect loomed over them. Her eyes widened in surprise at running into Nev, then narrowed as she glanced at the slightly askew stack of books behind them.

"Guinevere," Patience said, her voice light and musical, "how nice to run into you here. Can I help you with something?"

"No," Nev said, trying to match her conversational tone. "I was just looking up a Latin primer for Professor Bellairs's class. I can't seem to get my head around the verb structures."

Patience stepped forward, forcing Nev to take a step back. The movement was casual, but Nev felt like Patience was herding them, cutting off any route of escape.

"I can help you with that. Languages are a specialty of mine. Why don't you take a seat?"

"That's all right," Nev said. "I wouldn't want to waste your time. I know you're busy, and—"

"I *insist*," Patience said. The airiness of her voice took on a brittle edge.

She moved closer. Nev stepped back again, putting the table between them. They could feel the pull, the instinct to give Patience what she wanted, the dread at the idea of disappointing her. After what Nev had just seen in the scrapbook, those feelings suddenly seemed a lot more sinister, an idea in their head that they hadn't put there.

Nev was good at sensing when something didn't fit.

"Look! This is perfect," Nev said, picking up one of the many reference books from Patience's stack. "Do you mind if I borrow this? Then I can just let you get back to your work."

Patience smiled kindly.

"Guinevere, I know you and I haven't spent as much time together as I'd like. I've been busy, and from what I hear, you've been busy too. But I hope we respect each other enough that you're not lying to my face right now."

There it was again. That wave of shame, crashing into Nev with the force of a blow. Nev pushed through it and found that they were suddenly very annoyed.

"Stop that," Nev said. "If you want honesty, then stop messing with my head."

Patience blinked, surprised, before breaking into a radiant smile.

In an instant, the feeling of guilt faded from Nev's mind like a headache, leaving them feeling giddy and light-headed.

"I *knew* you were special," Patience said. "I'm glad we can finally be truthful with each other. Honesty is the foundation of any good friendship. Sit. Let's talk."

Nev settled uneasily into the armchair while Patience fetched a small wooden chair from a neighboring alcove. She sat across the table from Nev, smiling at her over the books, like a cat that knew the mouse was cornered.

"Now," Patience said, "why don't you tell me exactly what you and the dashing Mr. Harper have been up to?"

Nev shoved their hands deep into their pockets, running their fingers nervously over their tools.

"Danny and I know what's in the east wing."

"Mostly dust and squirrels these days, I expect."

Nev raised an eyebrow.

"I thought we weren't lying to each other."

"Very well," Patience sighed. "So you've found out about my, ah, earlier mistake."

"She nearly clawed me and Danny to shreds."

Patience shook her head, the gesture seeming to contain some genuine sadness.

"That's why I asked the principal to seal off the east wing, to string it up with bells, until I could find a solution. Naomi can't bear the sound of bells in her current state, you know."

"Why?" Nev said. They remembered the beast had screamed when Ruth rang her bell. If they ended up having to go back into the east wing, it would be good to have a defense.

"It's a side effect of the binding," Patience said. "The ringing of a bell was part of the original ritual. It was meant to be a kind of fail-safe, a way to protect myself in case things got out of hand. Which, as you know, they did."

Nev felt breathless, listening to Patience so casually describe the terrible thing that had happened to her classmate.

"Why, Patience? What were you trying to do?"

Patience shook her head, her pale gold hair swishing beautifully around her face.

"I think I've been very up front with you so far, but this is a conversation, not an interview. How about you answer some of my questions?"

Nev hunched farther into their jacket, feeling defensive.

"What questions?"

"*Quid pro quo*," Patience said. "Are you far enough in your Latin to know that one? 'This for that.' You answer a question of mine, and I'll answer one of yours. Fair?"

Nev took a second to think. It might be fair, but it

certainly wasn't safe. They were beginning to have an idea of what Patience was capable of.

They nodded.

"Good. My turn."

From inside her trim blazer, Patience produced the small, battered black journal.

"Where did you get this?"

Nev's eyes narrowed.

"Is that why you broke into my room?"

"Ah-ah. My turn, remember? Where?"

Nev hesitated again. Did Patience already know about the under-basement? If not, given what Nev had learned, they didn't want to be the one to tell her about it.

"I found it," they said. "It looked like it had been confiscated from another student, years ago. I don't know who or why."

Patience crooked an eyebrow.

"Was there more like this?"

"It's my turn," Nev said. "What was the ritual supposed to do?"

Patience sighed.

"It was an experiment, just a game. I'd found something in the library, scraps of a journal, and I translated them for fun. It was a ritual that would supposedly allow a person to change their shape. I thought a wolf would be classic. But I wasn't going to try it on myself, naturally, and Naomi was good enough to volunteer. You may have noticed, but people *love* doing things for me."

Patience leaned forward, smiling as she propped her elbows on the table and lacing her fingers below her chin.

"Does the principal know about your little adventures?"

"Yes, though I don't know how much," Nev said. They didn't see any way their answer could get them into more trouble than they were already in. "She threatened to expel me."

"I'd take that threat seriously, if I were you. Principal Blanchly is not one to shield students from the consequences of their actions. Be careful, Guinevere. We're just getting to know each other, and it would be a shame to lose you so soon."

The hungry gleam in Patience's eyes made Nev shiver.

"How much does the principal know about all of this?" they asked. "Does she know what you did to Naomi?"

"I don't think there's a lot that goes on in this house that Principal Blanchly *doesn't* know about. She seems to have her ways, just like I have mine."

"So why doesn't she do anything? Why doesn't she *fix* this?"

Patience shrugged.

"Maybe she simply doesn't *want* to do something. She might think of it as a learning experience. Or maybe she *can't*. What's done can't be undone."

She said this like she was quoting something, as if it were a law written in stone.

"In any case," Patience continued, "I've done what I can, and the principal has seen to the rest."

"So that's it?" Nev said. "You're just done? You don't think you're responsible?"

Patience frowned.

"I don't like making mistakes, Guinevere, but I own them when I do. Yes, I'm responsible for what happened. But I was younger and inexperienced. I thought it was just a game. I had only just begun to scratch the surface of this house's secrets. How could I have known such a thing was even *possible*? How could I have guessed what terrible, *wonderful* things this academy is hiding?"

She shook her head, laughing to herself.

"But you've managed to get a free question out of me. It's my turn again. Be honest, *why* are you so invested in digging up Deephaven's secrets? You could just keep your head down like a good little student."

"You're *collecting* those secrets," Nev said, nodding to the scrapbook.

"And you aren't?" Patience said, that hungry, eager gleam back in her eyes. She waved the journal again like it was evidence in a trial.

"With all your sneaking about and leading questions. Admit it, you want what this house has to offer as badly as I do."

"Patience, these things are *dangerous*—"

Patience laughed, loudly enough to earn a dirty look from the librarian.

"Of *course* it's dangerous. It's messy and strange and brutal. Did you expect it to be pretty? Pretty is for hair and clothes, Guinevere. This is *magic*. Magic is wonderful, yes, and powerful, but *never* pretty."

She smiled at Nev, her eyebrows furrowing in something like pity.

"Oh, come on. I've read your admissions file, Guinevere Tallow. One of the privileges of being a prefect. I know what you've come from."

She reached forward, taking Nev's hands in her own, her grip tightening when Nev tried to pull away.

"I'm on my own too, you know. The world would kick people like you and me to the curb and expect us to smile with gratitude at whatever scraps we find there. But that won't ever be enough for us, will it?"

Nev frowned.

"If you read my file," they said, "then you know I'm *not* like you. I'm not rich or well-connected. I don't have power. I don't *want* it. I'm not here for any of that. I'm just trying to get on with my life."

Patience's smile shifted into something sad, almost motherly.

"Oh, Guinevere. You don't have to lie to me, and you don't have to lie to yourself. Not here, not anymore. *Everyone* wants power. '*Potentiale est Potentia*,' remember? 'Potential is Power.' The power to be free, to shape your own future however you want it. That's all *this* is."

She moved the books in the stack aside, patting the green canvas cover of her scrapbook.

"Be honest. Aren't you tired of not having a choice, of being scared all the time? I *do* know you, Guinevere. You want control."

Nev fidgeted in their seat. They told themself it was Patience's intensity that was making them uncomfortable.

"I don't," they said. "Not like this. Not if it means trapping an innocent girl in a monster's skin."

Patience flinched, her smile cracking.

"I told you, that was a mistake—"

"Then help me *fix* it," Nev said. "Help me find a

way to undo all of this."

"You don't think I've tried?"

Patience thrust her scrapbook between them, flipping roughly through the pages.

"I've learned *so many* things, Guinevere. I've learned how to speak with spirits, how to craft dreams, and yes, how to make monsters. But in all I've read and all I've seen, I've *never* learned how to undo something that has been done."

"There has to be a way," Nev said.

"You sound like Ruth. She's always after me to look harder, go farther for a solution. She's *obsessed*. Our little séance was her idea, you know."

Nev remembered Ruth's iron grip on their hand, unyielding as the thing in the dark drew close. Nev shivered.

"What *was* that?" Nev asked.

"Ruth was afraid that one of you had run into poor Naomi," Patience said. "She was afraid you might do something *drastic*. Of course, we couldn't just *ask* you. What if you hadn't seen anything? A curious mind like yours, you would have marched into the east wing on your own straightaway."

She flipped to a spread in her scrapbook. There was a printed page from a book, long since torn from its spine. On it was an old-fashioned etching showing people in suits seated in a circle around a table, hands joined, a candle flame and a single flower in the center.

"I had a new game I'd been wanting to try. Spirits will tell you all kinds of useful things if you know how to ask them politely."

That black shape in the darkness, reaching for them, eager and hungry.

"What did it tell you?" Nev said.

Patience waved her hand dismissively.

"Nothing. Someone in the circle chickened out before we could finish our conversation. Ruth must have had second thoughts."

Nev reached out to page through the scrapbook that Patience had left in front of them. Patience made no move to stop them, merely watching them with interest.

"Ruth is the one being reckless now," Nev said. They turned back to the pages that held the scraps of the small, yellowed notebook, reexamining them. "She's trying to let Naomi out of the east wing."

"What?" Patience's smile slowly faded from her face, leaving it blank. "S-she wouldn't be that foolish."

It was the first time Nev had seen Patience look rattled.

"I guess she got tired of waiting for you to fix your mistakes," Nev said coldly.

"I told you, there is *no way* to change it," Patience said.

"I can try," Nev said. They placed their hand on the scrapbook. "Let me borrow this. If you won't fix this, then at least let me try to fix it for you."

Patience laughed.

"What makes you think you can? I've been elbow-deep in this for a while now, Guinevere. You just got here. Why would you succeed when I couldn't?"

Nev looked at her evenly. "I'm *really* good at solving puzzles."

Patience arched an eyebrow. "Show me."

She nudged the scrapbook closer to Nev.

Nev flipped back and forth between the pages. Could they actually do this? It's true that they were good at puzzles, but puzzles relied on logic. Puzzles needed a set of assumptions about the way the world worked that were consistently, demonstrably true.

But this was different. This took Nev's understandable, solvable world and dissolved it into mist. This was *magic*.

Nev's eyes ran over the notes, the diagrams, the formulas. Their mechanical mind sorted the pieces, looking for patterns and fitting them together, just like with their toys. Without thinking, Nev pulled a spool of twine from their outer upper-right pocket, twisting it through their fingers.

They studied Patience's diagrams, the ones depicting the braids and knots that at that moment were wound with hair around three jagged teeth in Nev's pocket.

There was something to this, some strange kind of pattern. Nev began to weave the twine back and forth, following that pattern, feeling the shape of the spell through their fingers. They could almost grasp it, the strange sense of it, right at the edge of their consciousness. It felt like a dream they could nearly, but not quite, remember. They chased that sense, that almost-instinct, weaving the twine around it to make it physical, understandable, real.

Nev felt it in the back of their head first, where the base of their skull met their spine. It was a distant crackling, all burned iron and blood. Their mind had found the pattern now, even if they couldn't map the shape of it. Nev's fingers wove faster and faster, caught in the pattern, and with each knot tied in the twine, the iron burn spread down their spine and into their body.

"Stop."

Nev jumped, their fingers fumbling the thread, tangling it into nonsense. The iron sense drained from their spine, leaving them shaky.

Nev suddenly realized that Patience's hand was on their wrist, and had been there for some time. Patience gazed at them with an expression of urgency and renewed interest.

"Stop," she said again. "You don't know what would happen if you finished that spell here. *I* don't know what would happen."

"I can fix it. I can save Naomi," Nev said, and this time their voice swelled with confidence.

"Guinevere, you just touched magic. I know you felt it because I felt it too. So I'll tell you again, and you *must* believe me this time, that the first rule of magic is that you *cannot undo what has been done.*"

"Then the worst that can happen is you're proven right," Nev said.

"Trust me, there are worse things," Patience said, but the smile reappeared on her face. "All right. I'll let you *borrow* my research. In return, I get to hang on to *this* for as long as I want."

She brandished the journal one more time before tucking it back inside her blazer. Nev felt a pang of loss as it vanished from sight.

They stood, gripping the scrapbook under their arm. Patience made no move to stop them. She just kept smiling that radiant, predatory smile.

"Good luck, Guinevere," she said. "I'll leave the

east wing door unlocked for you. And I expect to get my book back. Now that you've tasted magic, you'll be tempted to hang on to it."

"I'll return it, I promise," Nev said. They could still feel the electric, invigorating crackle at the base of their skull.

"You'd better," Patience said. "Remember, what I did to Naomi was an accident. Imagine what I could do to you on *purpose*."

Chapter Fourteen

For all their confident words with Patience, now that the buzz of the magic had faded from the base of Nev's skull, they had to admit they had no idea what they were doing. It was all well and good to be able to call supernatural forces at will, but what would they do with it? How could they control it? Who's to say they wouldn't end up behaving as recklessly as Patience had?

Dinnertime came as the sun sank behind the surrounding hills, but Nev found they weren't hungry. The things they'd learned about the house, and the way the world worked, made things like eating seem silly. They felt buzzy and restless, a clockwork spring wound too tightly and in need of release.

In the end, they decided to remain in the library. Nev tucked into the most remote corner they could find on the upper floor, blocked off from the rest of the library by a large shelf and lit by a single gas lamp. They settled into the lone rickety chair placed there and opened Patience's scrapbook on the small study table nearby.

They scanned each corner of each page, studying every collected artifact and scrutinizing every note. It wasn't easy, and none of the information seemed to stick in Nev's head. It was so different from the world as Nev understood it. Their mechanical mind recoiled from the weirdness of what they were reading.

Without thinking about it, Nev began pulling mechanical components from their pockets, placing them on the table next to the scrapbook in tidy rows. It helped them to have their hands occupied while their mind worked. As their eyes scanned the dense pages, their hands began to assemble the components. Gears slotted along axles, bits of wire bound to metal casings. An unconscious object began to assemble under Nev's fingers, calming their mind as they continued to sift through the occult strangeness of the scrapbook.

Slowly, distantly, the feeling of burning iron and blood began to sizzle up their spine.

Nev read more smoothly as their fingers worked faster. The things in the scrapbook *almost* made sense, if Nev thought about them sideways. It was chaos contained with ritual. The object in Nev's hands began to take shape, their fingers a blur across the metal.

The iron burn spread within their skull, wiping out the need for solid logic.

It was there, the how and why of it all, of everything, right *there* within reach. They only needed to finish the patterns, to complete the ritual—

"Tallow, isn't it?"

The sudden voice made Nev jump. Their attention slammed back to the world around them, and they had a brief glimpse of a complex mechanical object, something like an astrolabe, forming between their fingers before it simply fell apart. The iron burn faded as the mechanical components lost their grip on each other, and Nev slumped back in their seat, suddenly exhausted.

They looked up to see the kindly, smiling face of Professor Tieran.

"I wouldn't do that here if I were you, dear."

The professor was wearing her customary oversized cardigan, her frizzy red and white hair practically glowing in the lamplight. She had a large stack of books under her arm.

"W-what?" Nev said.

They felt disoriented and strangely guilty, as if they'd been caught stealing. Professor Tieran only smiled.

"That all seems a bit advanced for you, don't you think? Though I admire your initiative."

"I'm sorry, I don't—sorry," Nev said.

They nervously swept the scattered screws and gears back into their jacket pockets. What had they been about to do? What had it looked like to Professor Tieran?

Tieran stepped closer to them, peering over at the scrapbook. Nev had to fight down the wild urge to sweep the scrapbook out of sight. It would only make them look more suspicious, and the professor might start asking some uncomfortable questions, or worse, confiscate the book.

"Higher engineering," Tieran said, a pleasant crackle in her voice. "Tricky. We don't teach that kind of thing here, of course; it's a bit too advanced for the age range. But it does overlap with theoretical mathematics."

She reached over, paging through the stiff spreads of the scrapbook. Nev looked apprehensively at the professor's face, at the frown that was deepening on it.

"Hmm," Tieran rumbled.

"Professor?"

"This all seems a bit disorganized, don't you think?" the professor said. "Granted, language isn't really my strong suit, so I can't make heads or tails of most of this. Are you collecting for a specific project?"

"It's, ah, not mine," Nev said.

"Well, whoever's it is, it could use a bit more structure. Look here—"

She tapped a finger against a page that looked like it had been torn from an ancient textbook, bearing a circle filled with complex, interlocking glyphs. Nev didn't understand any of it, but the way the symbols fit together reminded them of the inner workings of a clock.

"This is incomplete," Tieran said. "It's a single application of a mathematical process, or a mechanical one, if it's easier for you to think of it that way."

Nev looked closer at the diagram, trying to see what the professor was seeing.

"How so?" they asked, the picture of a diligent student.

"Well, look here. It's structured to only allow for a single function. Only one logical outcome. It would be like if you invented a wheel that could only spin one way."

She shook her head, her fiery hair bobbing.

"Better than nothing, I suppose, but functionally useless. If you could introduce more variables, you'd have the possibility for more outcomes."

Nev's mechanical mind caught on the professor's words. Introducing more variables meant more outcomes. Different outcomes meant more ways a spell could be used.

Their mind shifted through the pattern that had transformed Naomi, even as their fingers twitched through its motions. In their mind, the part of Nev that needed to solve puzzles introduced a new thread.

They knew how to change the pattern.

Nev looked up at Professor Tieran and smiled.

"Thank you, Professor. That's very helpful."

Professor Tieran returned the smile, though it looked confused on her face.

"Oh, it's no problem. It's my job, after all. Well, good luck with . . . whatever it is you're working on."

Nev closed the scrapbook, gathering the remainder of their things. They needed to find Danny.

"Tallow?"

Nev looked up to see Professor Tieran still smiling at them, though there seemed to be something almost sad about the expression.

"Yes, Professor?"

"Ambition is encouraged, but just make sure your reach doesn't exceed your grasp, won't you?"

Nev studied the professor's expression, trying unsuccessfully to glean her meaning. People and their emotions weren't Nev's strong suit. Danny was much better at that kind of thing.

"Of course, Professor," they finally said.

Professor Tieran nodded, apparently satisfied, and returned to searching the nearby shelves.

Nev hurried out of the comfortable, amber-lit gloom of the library to find Danny, the beginnings of a plan forming in their head.

༒

"You want to do the ritual *again*?"

Danny sat sideways on the wood chair at Nev's desk, looking at them incredulously. Nev perched on the edge of their bed, the scrapbook open on their lap. They glanced up from Patience's notes.

"Exactly. Patience said that we can't undo what's been done. I don't know if she's right, but we don't have time to figure it out. I haven't seen Ruth today, and if she's still in the east wing, then she *and* Naomi are in danger."

"So you think we can do the same spell to turn Naomi human instead?"

Nev drew the small leather pouch from their pocket.

"We already have most of what we need. A piece of what we *want* her to be—a strand of her hair—and a bell for the catalyst."

Nev drew out a small, silvery hand bell that they'd taken from the dining room.

"All we need is a piece of what she is *now* to bind to it. That's the tricky part."

Danny lapsed into silence, thinking.

"If Ruth is still in the east wing," he said slowly, "and she's all right, she could help with that."

"When I saw her in there, she was . . . protective. She won't want to help us."

"She will," Danny said. "Trust me. You don't put yourself in that much danger unless you really care about someone."

"All right," Nev said. They still weren't sure they could rely on Ruth's help, but they were willing to rely on Danny's better intuition with people. "Once we've got a piece of the beast's hair, I'll need time to do the ritual. It won't take long, but . . ."

Danny sighed.

"You'll need a distraction."

Nev nodded grimly.

Danny stood and walked out of Nev's room without a word, a resolute look on his face. For a long minute, Nev thought they'd asked too much of him and had made him angry.

Then Danny returned with an ancient-looking rapier in his hand. It wasn't like the fencing foil he used at practice; this was an actual sword.

He swished the blade upright in a salute.

"If I'm going to have to face the beast again, I'll need to be able to hold my own. Just in case."

"Where did you get that?" Nev said, their face split between shock and a smile. They thought Danny cut a dashing figure in the doorway.

"From the display over the common-room mantelpiece," he said, his face breaking into a grin. "I think it's an antique. We'd better get out of this alive, or the principal is going to be really upset that I didn't put this back."

He slid the rapier into the loop of his suspenders before reaching out a hand to Nev, helping them stand up from the bed.

"Ready to face the beast of the east wing?"

Chapter Fifteen

"This is a terrible idea," Danny said.

They were standing in the dark, staring at the door of the east wing. The cord of bells remained strung across the entrance, a strange lock to secure a strange prisoner.

"The idea was partially yours," Nev said.

"I know," Danny said, "and it's a terrible one."

Nev gave him the most encouraging smile they could muster. Then, before they could have a moment longer to second-guess it, they gently pulled the cord of bells from the doorframe by the loose nail, like they'd seen Thaddeus do. They managed to pull the bells away with barely a sound. True to Patience's word, the padlock on the heavy door was unlocked, and the door swung open.

Nev shifted the small bag they had slung from their shoulder. It contained Patience's scrapbook, a pair of scissors, the small bell, and a battered silver pocket watch casing. Nev had removed the innards of the broken watch, making room within the make-shift locket for the black twist of knotted hair. If their plan worked, the three teeth that the hair had been wrapped around would no longer be needed, but they were tucked in their jacket's inner middle-left pocket, just in case.

Nev looked at Danny, and the two gave each other a silent nod. They were as prepared as they were going to be.

Together, they padded into the stillness of the east wing. Melted down candle stubs from the night they'd been locked into the tower still littered parts of the floor. Nev searched the shadows, looking for a glimpse of gleaming blue eyes or teeth or fangs. There was only dust and cobwebs. Nev shut the door softly, using the dead bolt to lock it from the inside. Danny walked ahead, his stolen rapier at the ready, leading them both up the winding stairs.

They moved with careful slowness. Nev strained

to hear past the sound of their own heart hammering in their ears, listening for any sign of the beast. If their plan was going to work, they needed to see Naomi before she saw them. Every step took Nev and Danny past an abandoned room or a shadowy corridor, each of them containing the possibility of the beast.

Then, at the very edge of Nev's hearing came the sound of humming. It drifted through the halls, so faint and fragmented it was like a dream slipping away upon waking. Nev wasn't entirely sure they were actually hearing it until Danny cast a curious glance at them. Nev nodded silently.

Ruth was still in the east wing, and she was still alive.

Danny and Nev went up another flight of stairs and were met with the now-familiar smell of burned iron and blood. Nev held their breath. They couldn't afford to retch.

In a large room at the far end of the curving hallway, a room that might have once been a prefect's suite, Ruth knelt in a pool of moonlight, humming softly. She must have snuck back out into the house at some point because her clothes had changed. She now wore a long black jacket and high boots, clothes for traveling. A packed bag rested behind her, and in front of her was a blanket with the remains of a midnight picnic. Curled in front of her, just outside the border of moonlight, the ragged black shape of Naomi's monstrous form rested. She breathed softly, soothed by the steady rhythm of Ruth's humming, her tangle of oily hair bleeding across the floorboards like spilled ink.

Danny lowered his sword but kept a tight grip on the hilt. Nev stepped into the room.

It was a moment before Ruth noticed them, and when she did, her gasp interrupted her humming and disquieted the beast resting on the floor. Naomi shifted uneasily, and a sound between a growl and a moan shivered through the floorboards.

"It's all right," Nev said softly. They held up their empty hands. "We're here to help you."

"You can't be here," Ruth hissed. Nev could tell she was trying to keep her voice under control, but Naomi sensed the sudden tension humming through it anyway. The long tangles of hair snarled up around her, and Nev could see the gleam of long white teeth in the dark.

Ruth stood slowly, her eyes wide with fear and fury.

"Leave, right now," she hissed through her teeth.

"Ruth—"

Nev took a step forward. At the movement, the dark shape on the floor uncoiled, blotting out the moonlight. The pale-fire points of Naomi's eyes blazed in the darkness, her elongated jaws snarling wide. Nev took a step back.

"Ruth, please."

Ruth shook her head. Her eyes darted between Nev and Naomi.

"No. Just go. You don't understand."

"I want to," Nev said. "I think I already do. I know who this is. I know that's Naomi."

Ruth froze. Naomi's gleaming eyes were trained on Nev, unblinking. Danny stepped gingerly from the doorway.

"We just want to help," Danny said. "We aren't going to hurt her."

"You *already* hurt her!"

Ruth's voice cracked, and the sound of the pain in it fed into the threat that Naomi clearly thought stood in front of her. She reached out with her shaggy, elongated limbs, her curving claws digging jagged trails into the floorboards. Nev and Danny both took another careful step back. Nev had no doubt that Naomi would rip them to shreds if she wasn't calmed, but even now, she no longer looked like a fearsome predator to Nev. She looked like something that had been viciously betrayed before and expected it would happen again.

"We can fix this," Nev said softly.

Ruth laughed, a soft and bitter sound. She stepped forward slowly until she was in Naomi's periphery. She began speaking, low and steady, soothing the beast.

"That's what Patience used to say. She doesn't say it anymore, of course. Now she just avoids me. She always wants people to play her little *games*, but never wants to deal with the consequences."

Naomi reacted to the steadying sound of Ruth's voice. The growling moan faded as she settled back. Ruth reached up slowly, running her fingers through the tangle of Naomi's hair. Naomi didn't blink. She continued to stare at Nev with her burning blue eyes.

"We used to go to Patience's parties all the time," Ruth continued. "Patience would have a new game, and we'd all get together to play it. It almost felt like being part of a family. We could pretend that they were normal games you play in the dark. Just like we pretended this was a normal school, not a place where we could be abandoned by the people who were supposed to love us."

"Ruth, tell me what happened," Nev said. They took a careful step back into the room. They would need to get close. Naomi's eyes didn't leave them, but she didn't move.

"Naomi thought it was great fun. She would do anything for Patience. She was *obsessed* with Patience. So when Patience said she needed a volunteer for a new game, Naomi couldn't be at her side fast enough."

Ruth kept her voice low and steady, but a wistful sadness had crept in around the edges.

"Patience said she needed some of her hair. Naomi had really pretty hair, all dark and curly. Patience snipped a bit off, just a strand, and *did something* with it. I couldn't really see. Then we blew out the lights, and when we lit them again, Naomi was supposed to be . . . something else. Just for a moment. But the lights were lit and she was still standing there. Nothing had happened."

Nev took a few more steps. They could feel Danny through the floorboards, keeping a slow pace behind them. They could sense his tension.

Ruth didn't notice them approach. She kept running her fingers through the tangle of Naomi's oily black hair, her eyes unfocused, lost in the memory.

"We all laughed at how scared we'd been for that moment in the dark, how silly it all was. I remember feeling sick, though. I remember tasting iron. We all went to bed like it was just another night. And then it happened."

Ruth took a shuddering breath, closing her eyes to calm herself.

"I'll never forget it. The *screaming*. It didn't sound human, the way it rang through the walls. I knew it was coming from Naomi's room, I just *knew*. I ran in there. It was dark, but I could see that it had been smashed up, and in the middle of it all, Naomi was—"

Ruth choked back a sob. The beast flinched at the noise, but Ruth kept combing her fingers through her hair, soothing her.

"They locked the place up, told everyone there had been an accident. They said the screams were the sound of the tower's support beams buckling. And everyone just believed it. They moved on, as if Naomi were actually gone. As if she didn't *matter*. But I knew better. I knew she was still here. I wouldn't abandon her."

Nev was close enough that they could almost see through the snarl of Naomi's black hair to her gray skin, stretched thin across her distorted face and elongated neck. Nev hoped it would be close enough.

They shifted the small bag they carried and drew out the scissors.

The silvery metal glinted in the moonlight. The gleam caught in Naomi's eyes and set them blazing. She whipped out her vicious claws faster than Nev's eyes could track, raking along Nev's arm and tearing at the skin of their hand. Nev cried out. The scissors were sent scattering across the floorboards and into the shadows.

Danny yanked Nev back by their shoulder, putting himself between them and Naomi. Naomi loomed over him, her long and twisted shape bent into a crouch, ready to spring.

"You *liars!*" Ruth cried. "You said you wouldn't hurt her!"

"We don't want to!" Nev said. They cradled their hand, flexing their fingers against the stinging pain. "Ruth, listen to me. There's a way to fix this. We can turn Naomi back into a girl again. We can *save* her!"

Ruth shook her head, stepping away from them and Naomi.

"No, you're lying. Patience said—"

"Never mind Patience," Danny said. He still hadn't raised his sword, holding it stiffly at his side. He didn't take his eyes from Naomi. "We can change the curse. We can make a *new* one!"

"W-what?" Ruth said.

Nev dug into the bag, pulling out the makeshift locket by the long silvery chain they'd strung through it.

"I can't undo it," Nev said, "so we'll do it again. A

spell to turn a beast into a girl. I already have the hair of the girl she should be, see?"

Nev flipped open the clasp, revealing the twist of hair inside.

"It's just like before. All the spell needs is hair from the thing she is now."

Ruth stared at Nev. Nev could see her indecision, the mistrust warring with her hope that there, at last, might be a way out.

"No," she said. "No, I don't believe you. I won't let you hurt her. I won't let anyone hurt her ever again!"

"Because you love her," Danny said.

His voice was calm, even as he stared steadily into the face of the fanged beast towering over him. Ruth's breath hitched.

"You're in love with her, I can see that," Danny continued steadily. "It's all right. We aren't going to hurt her, Ruth."

"Please," Nev said. They could see the silvery outline of the scissors on the floor, just behind where Ruth was standing. "Naomi trusts you. Help us end this. Help us save her."

Ruth stared at Nev, her eyes wide and her hands pressed over her mouth. Naomi took a long step forward, her moaning growl rising again to rumble the floorboards. Danny took a stumbling step backward, fighting his instinct to raise his weapon even as the beast's maw drew close.

"N-Naomi!"

The beast stopped at the sound of Ruth's voice, swiveling her head around, her eyes still blazing furiously.

"It's all right," Ruth said. She kept her voice low and kept her eyes on Naomi. She stepped carefully backward and crouched, feeling around for the scissors.

"It's going to be all right," Ruth said again. Her words came constant and rhythmic again, a handler soothing a startled beast, or a girl comforting her frightened friend.

The beast's teeth were still bared; her claws still tore anxiously into the wood of the floor. But she didn't move.

Ruth gripped the scissors so tightly her knuckles went white. She held them so that only the rounded metal handles were visible from under her sleeve. She took one step toward Naomi, then another. Nev and Danny didn't dare move, didn't dare breathe, afraid to break the spell of the beast's silence.

"Trust me," Ruth continued. "You've always trusted me, haven't you? Trust me one more time, and then it will be done. Then you can finally wake up from this nightmare. You can finally come back to me."

She reached out, grazing the edges of the beast's twisted hair with the tips of her fingers. Naomi shuddered, eyes wide and blazing, but she still didn't move.

"Oh, Naomi," Ruth breathed. "I miss you so much."

She ran her fingers through the inky black strands of hair, keeping one held loosely between her fingers. With her other hand, she brought the scissors into the moonlight, opening them with a soft *snikt*.

That's when they all heard the door to the east wing get kicked in.

Chapter Sixteen

The house shuddered like a wounded animal at the intrusion as the crash from far below rippled up the tower. Naomi snarled viciously in response, her eyes blazing brighter with terror and violence. Ruth scrambled backward, the scissors hanging open by her side.

"No, no!" she said. "Not yet! Not now!"

Naomi took one long step toward her, her gray, wolfish lips pulling back from long white fangs.

"Naomi, please . . ."

Nev stood paralyzed, their face aghast.

"Ruth, what did you do?"

248

Ruth sobbed.

"I couldn't wait any longer. Patience wasn't going to help. She was *never* going to help. I *had* to at least free Naomi from this place. So I asked someone else."

At the edge of Nev's hearing, barely discernible through the rattle of Naomi's growl, they could hear Thaddeus cursing.

Danny looked at Ruth in panic and disbelief.

"You asked *Thaddeus* for help? *Him?!*"

Naomi's snarl grew in pitch until it reached a furious scream. She reached out her long, shaggy limbs for Ruth and lunged, jaws gaping wide.

The scream turned to a startled yelp as Danny threw himself at the beast, knocking her off-balance and sending her crashing to the floor.

"Don't hurt her!" Ruth cried.

"Come on!" Nev said, grabbing Ruth by the elbow, dragging her out of Naomi's reach and into the hall, Danny stumbling quickly behind them. Naomi crawled after, screeching terribly.

Nev managed to slam the door to the room shut just as Naomi's onyx claws swept out. They heard the claws cut into the wood and felt the door tremble as they leaned their back against it. Danny pushed against the door beside them as it began to buck violently.

"I-I didn't tell him anything," Ruth said, tears streaming down her stricken face. "I just needed him to unlock the door so I could lead her out. She won't leave, she won't go through the windows. I just said he'd find Patience's secret here. H-he's always—"

"We have to get rid of him," Nev said. "Ruth, you know Thaddeus won't help once he knows what is locked up in here. I don't know what he'll do, but if he *sees* her, things will only get worse."

Ruth nodded, hiccupping through tears. Danny nudged Nev's shoulder.

"Go," he said. "I'll stay here with Ruth. Maybe we can calm Naomi."

Nev opened their mouth to protest, but already they could see the strain on Danny's face and feel the splintering of the wood behind them.

They didn't have much time.

Nev nodded to Ruth. Ruth wiped her coat sleeve across her face and switched places with Nev, joining Danny in holding the door shut. Nev set off down the hall at a run.

The wheels of their mind were already spinning fast, churning through the wreckage of their plan and trying to craft the pieces into a new one. They had to make Thaddeus leave, that was the first thing. He was going to get somebody killed, possibly himself. He couldn't know what was in the east wing. Nev didn't know what Thaddeus would do with the knowledge of what had become of Naomi, but they were sure it wouldn't be good. Nev also couldn't be seen. If they survived the night, and they certainly hoped to, they couldn't let word get back to Principal Blanchly, or Nev would be averting the immediate crisis only to be turned out into the cold.

"Hello?" Thaddeus's voice drifted faintly from below. Nev hoped that he couldn't hear the commotion above. Though, now that they thought about it, they couldn't hear anything anymore either. They hoped that was a good sign.

"Rose, or whatever your name is," Thaddeus said, "where are you? If this is some kind of trick, I swear you'll regret it."

Nev slowed their pace, stepping softly to muffle the sound of their footsteps. Even so, the house creaked around them, noting their presence. Thaddeus must have heard the sound because his voice choked off suddenly.

"I-is that you? Patience is with you, isn't she? You won't scare me. I-I don't believe in those *stupid* stories we tell the first-years. There *are* no ghosts, I *know* there aren't."

Nev didn't move, not wanting to further alert Thaddeus to their presence. They stood in a long hallway on the second floor. At the far end, they could just see the faint amber glow of a candle as Thaddeus began to move up the stairs.

There was a note of fear in Thaddeus's voice. Nev could hear how scared he was, no matter what he said. The wheels in their mind continued to turn, and a new plan started to click into place.

It was even more terrible than the last plan.

Nev ducked into a shadowy alcove and crouched out of sight. They pulled Patience's scrapbook from the bag and began to flip furiously through the pages, squinting at the pale ink handwriting in the darkness.

"You think you're so clever," Thaddeus said, "with your little parties and your ghost stories. But I *know* you're hiding something in here. I'm going to find it, and then we'll see if the principal still likes you so much."

Nev could hear his footsteps now, the *clack-clack-clack* as he reached the top of the stairs. They didn't peer out of their hiding place to look, instead focusing on the dim page open in front of them and its notes on candles and flowers and blood.

Thaddeus was scared of ghosts. After all, the east wing was supposed to be haunted, wasn't it? Nev thought they could meet his expectations.

"This is ridiculous," Thaddeus said. "I-it's sad, really. You have to play these games to keep yourself in the academy's good graces, to hang on to this last shred of power. It's pathetic. I'm going to expose you, and then you'll see. Things will change. Then I'll be the favorite; *I'll* be the one running things."

Nev ignored him. Patience's book said that the ritual required human blood to lure the spirit, along with living tissue, like a flower, to keep it there. Nev didn't have a flower. They hoped their blood would be enough. They didn't want the spirit to stay long, anyway.

Nev pushed farther into the shadows of the alcove as the outer edges of the light from Thaddeus's candle dusted the floorboards.

It was time to play a dangerous game.

Nev dug into the inner upper-left pocket of their coat and drew out a fountain pen. They dug the sharp pen nib into the pad of their finger, sucking in a silent breath at the bright spark of pain. They pressed until a dark, wet spot bloomed beneath the pen, ink mixing with their blood.

"I-I can hear you!" Thaddeus called. Nev could no longer hear footsteps; Thaddeus stood rooted to the spot in the darkened hallway, fear spilling into his voice. "Come out! It'll go easier for you if you come out now."

Now came the tricky part. Nev fumbled in their pocket for the box of matches. They were certain that Thaddeus would be able to see the light once it was struck, but they hoped that he would either be too slow or too scared to reach their hiding place before Nev could do what needed to be done.

They struck the match, setting it to blazing life.

"Who is that?!" Thaddeus cried. His voice was high and startled. "I can see you!"

His footsteps started down the hallway, their pace quick but faltering. Nev cursed inwardly. They held the lit match in one hand and held out their bloodied finger with the other.

The blood calls.
The flame guides.
The bloom stalls.
The soul confides.

Nev repeated the chant in a frantic whisper, keeping hurried time with the *clack* of Thaddeus's approaching heels across the floor.

"You don't want to play games with me. I'm a *Cuttingham!*"

Just as the light from Thaddeus's candle caught the edge of Nev's boot, the stale air of the tower came alive.

An electric feeling hummed through the tower, like the air before a storm. Icy pain spiked through Nev's bloodied finger and down into their arm. They nearly cried out, choking back the scream as the pain quickly spread into a chill numbness. Darkness gathered around the match flame and spread.

"W-what—" Thaddeus whimpered as he scrambled back, away from where Nev crouched.

The house groaned painfully around them, twisted by the invading presence that now towered in the middle of the hallway.

What little light still existed from the match bent itself toward the vaguely human shape of the figure, vanishing into the negative hollow of its silhouette like starlight being swallowed by a black hole. It turned its empty face upon Nev, ignoring its surroundings.

There was no expression on the thing's lack of a face, but Nev knew it recognized them. It had been waiting for their call.

Distantly, Nev heard Thaddeus make a sad, choking sound. The thing towering above them didn't take notice, not even seeming to register his presence. It came closer to Nev without moving, the house simply warping around it. Nev's hair stood on end in the crackling atmosphere. Their arm, which they suddenly realized was outstretched toward the thing, throbbed distantly.

The shape reached out to them, its movements slow, almost gentle. Nev could feel its emptiness and hunger. It extended a long tendril of an arm to Nev's outstretched finger, eager for the life that flowed through them and bled out into the open air. Nev gasped as the numbness in their arm spread up and into their chest, slowing their heartbeat to a sluggish crawl.

Nev understood, with the detachment of a dream, that they were dying.

With a titanic effort, Nev pulled their gaze away from the consuming emptiness of the thing's face. They struggled to draw a breath, their chest tight as if they'd been plunged into icy waters. With a fierce, desperate gasp, Nev blew the match flame out.

Just like that, the thing in the hall was gone. The house let out a shuddering breath just as Nev gulped one in. The hall stood with an emptiness that had no desire to consume, only to be left still.

Thaddeus was nowhere in sight.

Nev unfolded painfully from the alcove, tucking the scrapbook back into their bag. Their arm ached.

They walked carefully to the end of the hall to

peer down the curve of the stairs and onto the ground floor lobby. Nev was just in time to see Thaddeus's terrified, stricken face as he stumbled over his own feet in his haste to flee. He scrambled at the east wing door and slammed it shut behind him with a resounding, panicked *bang*.

If Thaddeus didn't believe the east wing was haunted before, he certainly did now.

Nev shivered, the sudden ache in their muscles crying out for rest, even as they turned back toward the depths of the tower.

The empty thing in the dark was gone, but the east wing was still haunted.

Nev took the stairs two at a time, hoping that the continuing silence from the floors above meant that Danny and Ruth had things under control. They let out a relieved sigh when they reached the door and found Danny seated on the ground with his legs braced for another assault from the other side. None came, the room within remaining still and silent. Ruth stood nearby, her shoulders hunched, the silver scissors gripped tight against her chest.

Danny's eyes lit up as Nev came around the bend of the hallway.

"You're okay! Did Thaddeus—"

"He's gone," Nev said. "He didn't see me."

"S-she's quiet," Ruth said. "She's waiting to see what we'll do. Maybe we should go. We'll come back when she's calmer—"

Nev shook their head.

"We won't have another chance. We've already drawn too much attention. It has to be tonight, right now."

Ruth's expression hardened, turning from panic to a fierce determination. She nodded silently. Danny stood up, sliding his back along the surface of the door. He nodded as well.

Without another word, they all took up positions in the hall. Ruth stood in the shadows beside the door, out of sight. Danny shifted his grip on his rapier to grasp the door handle, ready to open it at Nev's signal. Nev took a few paces back, standing in a patch of moonlight in the middle of the hall, the first and only person that Naomi would see when the door opened.

Nev gripped the makeshift locket, its chain glittering in the dark. They took a single, steadying breath, and nodded to Danny. Danny's lips drew into a tight line.

He pulled open the door.

A storm of hair and teeth exploded out into the hall, rushing toward Nev. Every instinct in Nev screamed for them to run, to do what any sensible creature would do in the face of a ravenous predator. Nev stood their ground, fighting the impulse as their senses were overwhelmed by the iron stench. The beast's tangled hair blotted out their vision. In the center of that jagged chaos were two cold pinpricks of light, burning furiously into Nev.

Nev didn't flinch.

Behind the terrible thing that had once been a girl, Ruth stepped from the shadows, scissors in hand.

"It's all right, Naomi. Everything will be all right now."

Nev spoke low and steady, mimicking the way Ruth had spoken earlier. Naomi slowed, her moaning growl uncertain.

"I'm a friend," Nev said. "I can't imagine what this has been like for you. You *are* still you in there, aren't you?"

Nev stood with their boots anchored to the floor. They held their hands away from their body, palms open, showing they held nothing but the locket dangling from its chain around their wrist.

Ruth reached out with the scissors ready, grasping softly at the edges of Naomi's long inky hair. Ruth wasn't breathing, her eyes unblinking with concentration.

"I know what it's like to be trapped, though," Nev

continued. "I know you're scared. It feels like everyone has abandoned you. It feels like no one will ever care enough to help."

The scissors opened slowly and silently, reaching toward the tangled strands of hair.

"But that's not true. We care. We're all *here*. You don't have to be alone anymore. You deserve to be rescued."

Snip.

It happened too fast for Nev to follow. One moment, the beast's burning eyes were locked with theirs. The next, startled by the noise, the beast whirled around in a blur of bared fangs and vicious claws, and Ruth was on the ground with her hands pressed against her face.

Blood oozed dark and slick from between Ruth's fingers as she began to scream.

The beast whirled back toward Nev, her jaws gaping wide as a monstrous wailing mingled with Ruth's screams.

"Hey!"

The beast whipped around again to face Danny, who had stepped from behind the door with his sword at the ready.

"No!" Ruth cried. Her blood-slick hands still covered her face, and her words sounded garbled, as though her mouth were suddenly ill-suited to forming the sounds. "Please don't hurt her!"

Danny hesitated for only a moment, but it was enough. Naomi's claws struck toward him, sinking into his leg. He cried out, falling backward as the beast dragged him close. Danny drove the pommel of his sword down into the back of Naomi's matted hand. She released him, pulling back with a pained hiss.

Nev ran to where Ruth knelt on the floor. There was a lot of blood. Nev had to glance away for a moment as their head spun at the sight.

"Here," Ruth croaked.

She held out her fist, releasing a long curl of inky hair into Nev's outstretched hand. Ruth clutched at her injured face, but her visible eye blazed bright and fierce.

"You have to finish this."

The hair felt oily and strangely dense against Nev's skin. Down the hallway, Naomi crouched low to the ground, ready to pounce. Danny stood shakily, holding his sword in a defensive stance.

Nev opened the locket and pulled out the hair within. They needed to work fast.

They laid open Patience's scrapbook on the floor in front of them, letting the moonlight illuminate the marked page, and set the small bell next to it. Nev's fingers worked deftly through the knots of Naomi's old hair, used to maneuvering small objects in precise ways. The hair felt dry and ephemeral against their fingers, and the strands soon lay open and unknotted beside the black curl of the beast's.

Some predatory sense in Naomi alerted her to vulnerable prey, and she turned back toward Nev as they knelt on the floor nearby. Danny struck the beast across the shoulder with the flat, whiplike edge of the blade, in a blow that wasn't intended to injure her but to recapture her attention. It worked, and Naomi twisted around with a snarl and slashed out with her claws. Danny brought the blade up in a parry. The beast's claws shrieked along the sword's metal, casting angry red sparks in the darkness.

Nev began to knot the black hair of the beast with the lighter hair of the girl the beast had once been, closely following the ornate pattern laid out in the scrapbook. Soon Nev could feel the rhythm of the knot, an instinctive logic that wove itself through their mind. There was no chanting, no other ritual, but Nev could feel that burned-metal sense crackle through their fingers and burn up their spine.

They reached for the bell and gave the first *ring*.

Out of the corner of their eye, they saw the black

shape of Naomi flinch in pain, but Nev didn't look away from the knot forming in their hands. They couldn't afford to be distracted.

As they twisted through the pattern, the world fell away. Part of Nev heard Danny grunt and the beast shriek. A crash. Ruth shouting a warning. A harsh scrape of metal on stone.

Holding the forming knot with one hand, Nev reached out and gave the bell a second *ring*.

Though shrieks and chaos stormed around them, Nev was unable to untangle their mind from the knot twisting between their fingers, caught in a pattern that could not be interrupted, only completed.

Ring.

Nev blinked, and the finished knot rested in their hands. The ornate swirls of hair twisted tightly in a small wreath. Nev looked up from the completed talisman to the scene in front of them.

Danny was tired, clearly exhausted from fending off Naomi's hungry claws with his uninjured arm. He sagged to one side, his face drawn and his shirt soaked with sweat. Ruth knelt on the floor near Nev, using the sash from her coat to bind a fistful of fabric to the side of her injured face.

The beast shook herself, dazed from the sound of the ringing bell. Her eyes burned with a renewed fury as she looked down at Danny and saw his weakness.

Nev couldn't think clearly. The metallic buzz that had shivered up their spine continued to build at the base of their skull. It hummed beneath their skin and made their muscles twitch. The ritual wasn't complete, not yet.

Naomi shivered as well, as if sensing the part of her that had been bound up anew in the talisman. The magic continued to bloom in Nev's bones, a building pressure that needed to be released.

Naomi howled in frustration and struck at Danny again. He held up his rapier weakly to block the blow, and the resounding shriek of claws on metal set Nev's teeth on edge. The claws hooked on the blade, ripping it from Danny's tired grasp and sending it skittering down the hall. Danny stumbled backward, shaking, as the beast surged forward with her jaws open wide.

Nev ran toward them, stuffing the talisman into the locket and closing it tight. They shoved their other hand deep into their pockets, grasping at something, anything that could help.

Their fingers closed around the smooth metal skeleton of the mechanical bird.

They pulled the unfinished toy free, winding it up with practiced motion. They set it on the ground and sent it soaring across the floorboards, the frame of its wings flapping manically. The beast's attention snapped toward the new intrusion, her burning eyes tracking the blur of movement across the floor.

Naomi reached toward the toy, leaning away from Danny. She stretched out her shaggy arm and smashed her claws down on the bird, sending fragments of metal and loose screws scattering into the dark corners of the hall.

"Naomi."

The beast turned at her name, right into where Nev stood. They were so close that all they could see was tangled hair, and the iron blood stench made tears stream from their eyes.

Naomi's head twisted toward them and slipped through the loop of chain that Nev held aloft.

Nev let go, letting the silvery chain vanish into the inky black of Naomi's hair until only the glint of the locket itself was visible. Naomi wrapped her long, clawed fingers around Nev's shoulders, pulling them toward her until Nev's vision filled with slick fangs and a black, roiling tongue. Then the beast's head whipped back painfully. Naomi screamed.

It was the most terrible sound that Nev had ever heard. The scream rattled through their bones and shook dust from the walls. Naomi's claws clutched desperately at Nev, tearing through their coat and dragging along their ribs.

Naomi's horrible scream continued, stretched to fill the space, and Nev screamed with her.

The ragged hair along the beast's arms twisted and writhed, as if an electric current passed through them. Her claws dug deeper into Nev's sides, making their vision blur from the pain.

Then, abruptly, Naomi let go. No, Nev thought dimly, that's not right. The claws didn't release, they *fell away*, dropping from Nev's side and from Naomi's arms.

The writhing of the beast's hair shivered into a boiling across its skin. Naomi's monstrous silhouette distorted and blurred. Matted hair and gleaming teeth all began to fall away, sloughing off like the skin of an overripe fruit. What remained of the beast pulled her arms tight against her chest as she continued to wail. The ragged form fell away, piling on the floor in matted clumps, revealing patches of smooth, pale skin.

The screaming faded, swallowed up by the hungry silence of the house.

In the beast's place crouched a girl.

Her head was down and her arms were pulled tightly across her chest. Pale, bare shoulders stood out against the long tangle of black, oily hair that hung down to cover most of her body, shivering among the

266

shed parts of the beast she had been made to be.

Ruth was the first to move. She brushed past Nev, holding the blanket she had used for the midnight picnics. She draped it across Naomi's shivering shoulders. Naomi flinched at the touch, but she drew the blanket more tightly around herself as she raised her head to look up at Ruth. Her eyes were wide and wild, dark rimmed and cold blue. Her face was long and pale, and around her neck was the gleam of a silvery chain.

"S-s-sor-r—"

Her voice was unsteady and unused, like a newborn animal that was still trying to find its legs.

Ruth wrapped her arms tightly around Naomi, who flinched again but didn't pull away.

"It's all right," Ruth said through her tears. "You have nothing to be sorry for. It's all right now, I've got you. I've got you, Naomi."

Nev stood, panting, a dull, stinging ache pulsing in their sides. Danny limped up to stand beside them. Neither of them said anything.

Crouched on the floor in front of them, Naomi's wide, frightened eyes finally closed. She relaxed into Ruth's embrace and began, softly, to cry.

The house murmured reassurances, gathering a soft stillness around the tired students.

267

Chapter Seventeen

"You understand that what you are asking for is highly irregular," Principal Blanchly said.

"But not unheard of," Nev said.

Nev sat in the principal's office, a place they hadn't been since their first day at Deephaven. Now, at the end of that first semester, the principal sat with her pen poised over a notebook, pausing to give Nev an even look over the top of her spectacles. It all felt so familiar.

"No," she said, "not unheard of."

Through the narrow lattice window that framed the principal, the first few drifting flakes of snow were visible. The house outside of the office was silent, save for its usual grumbling, a stark contrast to the commotion earlier in the day as students scurried around with last-minute packing and saying goodbye to their friends as they headed home for the winter break.

Most of the population of Deephaven was gone now, having been picked up by private chauffeurs or ferried in small groups into town and the train station. Only a few stragglers, like Nev, remained.

Principal Blanchly laid down her pen, steepled her slender, bony fingers, and pinned Nev with her critical gaze. Nev met her stare and tried not to squirm.

"*If* I agree, you will assume a fair amount of responsibility in maintaining the house. And you would be directly answerable to Prefect Sleepwell."

Nev swallowed. They didn't like giving Patience that much control, but they had already thought long and hard about their choice.

"I understand."

Blanchly's stare intensified.

"Be sure, Tallow. You won't be able to change your mind later."

Nev was sure. Their expression remained resolute. It must have been enough to satisfy the principal, because she gave a small sigh and a curt nod.

"Very well," she said, "I'll make the necessary arrangements. You can discuss details with Prefect Sleepwell later."

"Thank you, ma'am," Nev said, trying not to let the flood of relief they were feeling spill over their face. They hurriedly stood to leave. There was more that needed to be done.

"Tallow."

Nev turned back. The principal's eyes gleamed brightly behind their spectacles with a look that said she knew much more than she was saying.

"Don't think I'm unaware of some of your *extra-curricular* activities. You would do well to keep your focus on your studies. Be careful."

Nev was shaken but not surprised. After all, the heavy rope of bells had disappeared from the east wing door some time ago, though a sturdy new padlock had been left in its place.

Without another word, Principal Blanchly took up her pen and resumed her work. Nev hurried out of the office and down the stairs, the principal's words following after them like a shadow.

Nev found Danny outside in the snow, heaving luggage into the back of the truck that had once carried

Nev to Deephaven. Danny wore a tan tweed coat with a furred collar, the hem hanging down to his knees. His breath fogged to mingle with the exhaust of the idling truck as he worked. His injured arm was mostly healed, though he still wrapped it to keep it stiff. He no longer needed the bandages around his legs, just as Nev no longer needed the ones that had been wrapped around their ribs. They had all survived, but not unscathed. Their night in the east wing would leave its scars.

Two other figures stood nearby, holding hands. Ruth wore a long dark coat and a knit green scarf. She sported a clean white wrapping around part of her face, obscuring a corner of her mouth and the place where her eye had been.

Some scars would be more terrible than others.

Holding her hand was a tall, thin figure in a pale blue cloak, her long, tangled tresses spilling from under the hood in a waterfall of ink.

Most of the students at Deephaven were unaware of Naomi's miraculous return from the dead. She was nervous, and still had difficulty being out in the open. She had hidden within Ruth's dormitory room, and if Ruth continued to spirit away extra portions of food as she always had, no one thought it was strange. Even now, Naomi pressed against Ruth, as if the wide-open world might sweep her away like a drowning girl out to sea without an anchor, never to be seen again.

Danny waved to Nev as they emerged from the house, their boots silent on the gravel drive, muffled by the thin layer of snow.

"You're just in time," Danny panted. He wiped a sleeve across his brow, sweating from the exertion despite the cold. "That's the last of them. We're all ready, I think. Where's your stuff?"

"Still in my room," Nev said. "I'm staying here."

Danny stared at them, open-mouthed. "You're *staying*? *Alone*?"

Nev shrugged. "Patience will be here."

Out of the corner of their eye, Nev saw Naomi shiver beneath her cloak.

"Then this will be our last chance to thank you," Ruth said. "Naomi and I won't be coming back after the winter break."

Nev nodded. They had anticipated this, but they still felt a pang. They had not had many friends in their life, and a part of them had begun to think that Ruth and Naomi could grow to be friends.

"I-I can't be here a-anymore," Naomi said.

Her voice was quiet and scratchy, still unused to forming human words and sounds. It was about as many words as Nev had heard her put together so far.

"What will you do?" Nev asked.

Ruth glanced at Naomi, circling her arm protectively around her waist. Naomi relaxed into the embrace, comforted at the feeling of being anchored.

"We'll be all right," Ruth said. "Naomi was never exactly *close* with her family. They still think she's dead. My family is long gone, but I've still got some money from their estate. We're going to stay with my aunt. She'll understand, and her place is out in the country. We need someplace quiet to wait until the world makes sense again."

Patience had been right in what she'd said to Nev when they'd first arrived: Deephaven had a type. It drew lonely and isolated students to it like moths to a comforting flame. Now, at least, Naomi and Ruth had been drawn to each other.

Naomi nodded a silent thanks to Nev and Danny before folding herself into the back seat of the truck, with Ruth following close behind. As Naomi climbed in, Nev caught a brief glimpse of a silver chain around her neck, the locket hidden somewhere beneath her cloak.

Naomi knew that talisman would have to be kept on her for the layers of magic to remain in harmony.

"Constant contact," the journal had said. It had to remain around her neck, always, in order for Naomi to keep herself together. The beast was still in there, buried beneath the skin of the girl, bound tight with magic.

Nev didn't know what would happen if Naomi ever took the locket off. They hoped she would never find out.

Danny didn't move toward the truck, continuing to gaze at Nev with concern growing in his eyes.

"Nev, are you sure about this?"

"For better or worse, Deephaven is my home now," Nev said. Now that everything was settled, they felt calm, almost secure. It was an unfamiliar feeling. "I want to learn as much about what it's still hiding as I can."

"I'm worried about you," Danny said. "What if you came to spend the holidays with my family instead?"

Nev laughed. "No offense, Danny, but from what you've told me about them, I think I'd rather spend the winter here with Patience."

"Fair enough." Danny laughed, but the worry didn't fade from his eyes.

Nev gave him their most comforting smile.

"I've not had a lot of choices in my life," Nev said,

"but I chose to come here to Deephaven. Now I'm choosing to stay."

"All right," Danny said. "Keep safe, and as soon as I'm back, I'll help you."

"Before you go, I have something for you," Nev said.

They dug into their outer lower-left pocket and pulled out a bird. Its feathers were a dense patchwork of deep blues and purples and greens, its marble eyes blazing a brilliant yellow. A small silvery windup key sprouted from between its wings.

Danny's eyes lit up.

"You finished it!"

"I *remade* it," Nev said. There was no salvaging what was left of their first try, still scattered among the dust of the east wing. "I wanted to make sure you had it before you left."

Danny took the bird, turning it over in his hands to admire the craftsmanship. He surged suddenly forward and engulfed Nev in a hug. Nev stiffened for a moment, unused to the gesture and its mechanics. They relaxed slowly and returned the embrace. The pieces all seemed to fit together well enough.

"I'll be back soon," Danny said. "Be careful, Nev."

"I will."

They would try, at least.

Danny climbed into the truck and slid in next to Ruth, the bright colors of the mechanical bird glowing from where it rested on his lap. The truck's driver glanced back from her seat to make sure the last of her cargo was secured before shifting into gear and pulling out of the drive.

Nev stood as the snow fell heavier, watching the silhouettes of their friends through the rear window of the truck as they drove away. Soon their shapes were lost to the trees and the haze of snow.

Nev drew in a deep breath of biting air, holding the chill in their lungs for a long moment before releasing it in a cloud to mingle with the winter mist. They turned back to the house, and Deephaven yawned open for them, welcoming them back into the shelter of its shadowy halls.

For Guinevere Tallow, it felt like coming home.

ACKNOWLEDGMENTS

Making this book is both something very different for me, as someone who up to this point has mostly worked in comics, and also the kind of story I've dreamed of working on since I was a child. There are a lot of people who helped me make it happen, and they deserve thanks.

First, thanks to my mother, who gave me my love of horror and mystery stories, and to my father, who always did the monster voices when he read to me and my siblings. Speaking of, thank you to Erika, Hannah, Cole, and Megan, for their constant support and enthusiasm, and for being fellow enjoyers of spookier stories.

I owe a debt to the writers of those stories, who spark my imagination and influenced this book; writers like Shirley Jackson, John Bellairs, M. R. James, and many more.

Massive thanks to my brilliant and hardworking literary agent, Stephen Barbara, who was more excited than anyone when I said I wanted to write an all-ages horror mystery series. Thank you to my clever and insightful editor, Karen Chaplin, who fought for this story and has been its champion every step of the way. Thanks to Molly Fehr, Erin Fitzsimmons, Allison Weintraub, and the entire editing and production staff at Quill Tree Books for their expertise and hard work in making this story book-shaped and beautiful.

I owe many thanks to Brandon Thorp, for his in-depth notes, long talks through the plot, and keeping me honest on writing retreats. Thanks also to Kat Howard, whose editorial work helped the story find its shape, and who generously let me lean on her fencing knowledge. Any factual errors about the sport that remain are my own.

Special thanks to Wendy Xu, Rebecca Mock, Carey Pietsch, Seth Persons, and Matthew Soler, who were the very first to wander Deephaven's halls and dive into its shadows with me. Go, Grims!

And, finally, the biggest of thanks to my husband, Matthew. He doesn't like scary stories, but he read nearly every draft of *Deephaven*, anyway, and without his wit, insight, encouragement, and support, this book would not exist. Thank you.